THERE'S THE RIGHT WA
AND THE ENVI

Lucifer sat at the head
to Tracking's report on th
upon reaching North Carolina. Suddenly, he ripped the head off of the department manager and threw him into the Pit. Decisive management, he thought.

Communicable Diseases was next on the agenda, but Lucifer pointed to Scumslag, just back from North Carolina. "You next," he said. "How is the Devil's Point project coming?"

Devil's Point was to be an amusement park built in North Carolina, offering one-of-a-kind amusements such as a live-action role-playing game park with special effects from Hell.

"Everything is ready to go," Scumslag said. "We've located the land we want. The only problem is that the owners won't sell."

"I don't recall much resistance from humans before," Lucifer said. "They've always been greedy little bastards."

"Yes, they have. But this particular plot of land happens to have fallen into the hands of people who aren't motivated by greed."

"Fundamentalists?" Lucifer scoffed. "They can be tempted."

"Oh, no, Your Horribleness. Much worse than Fundamentalists. *Environ*mentalists."

The fallen angels around the table hissed, and even Lucifer made the sign of the evil eye. "Find another piece of land," Lucifer said. "You'll never get their nasty little claws out of that one."

"But I think I will." Scumslag's smile grew huge. "Greed won't get them, but I think their politically correct agenda will. They want the power to force other people to do things their way or no way at all. So I'm working on that angle. I'll get 'em."

Also by Holly Lisle

Fire in the Mist
Bones of the Past
Mind of the Magic

Minerva Wakes
Sympathy for the Devil
When the Bough Breaks
with Mercedes Lackey
The Rose Sea
with S.M. Stirling
Mall, Mayhem & Magic
with Chris Guin

HOLLY LISLE

The Devil & Dan Cooley

WALTER SPENCE

BAEN

THE DEVIL AND DAN COOLEY

A Baen Books Original

Baen Publishing Enterprises
P.O. Box 1403
Riverdale, NY 10471

ISBN: 0-671-87756-9

Cover art by Clyde Caldwell

First printing, December 1996

Distributed by Simon & Schuster
1230 Avenue of the Americas
New York, NY 10020

Printed in the United States of America

In Memory of
James Owen Spence

H.L. & W.L.S.

Chapter 1

TUESDAY, JUNE 7TH

God's pager chimed the first couple of bars of Pachelbel's Canon and Gigue in D major. That meant Heaven calling . . . again. God frowned and switched off her pager—lately most of her problems came from Heaven. She wondered if she could just let this one go for a while, pretend she'd been too busy to notice the beeper at all, maybe even answer by e-mail instead of with a personal visitation. Off to one side of her, the Maypole dancers wove in and out around each other, swirling and skipping in their ethereal robes to the beat of an extraordinary drummer and the piping of the original Pan. It was going to be a great party. The folks in the pagan afterlife always threw great parties.

But Honorial, Heaven's Chief Recording Angel of Data Processing, never called unless he had an honest-to-God emergency. Maybe, God thought, this will just be a little one. Maybe I'll be able to handle the trouble in Heaven and get back to Summerland in time for the buffet.

God switched out of Goddess mode into the long-bearded persona his Christian children overwhelmingly preferred (he forgot once when he left Mt. Olympus and went through the pearly gates as Zeus, but nobody noticed) and slipped into Heaven, the Christian neighborhood of the afterlife.

As he came through the doors, Heaven's choirs finished up some brand new Bach and switched to rock and roll, with Elvis doing the lead vocals. Elvis sounded great. That short stint in Hell before he repented had been better for him than the Army, and had given him some new themes to write about.

God liked the new song; he snapped his fingers and bopped with the beat. By the time he reached his recording angel, who sat frowning at the computer screen, he was singing along with the chorus.

> Cause buh-buh-buh-baby I don'ah like it—
> No, no, no, no, I don' like it—
> Oh, baby, I don' like it—
> Where it's hot!

Honorial sighed. God remembered a bit too late that Honorial much preferred Gregorian chants and madrigals to any other music, and considered more recent styles discordant. He quit singing and surrounded the two of them with silence.

"Problems?"

"Yes, Almighty. The numbers on Operation Tarheel just came in and they aren't good."

"They aren't?" That came as a surprise, and things rarely surprised God. He leaned over the angel's shoulder and looked at the monitor. Honorial brought up the North Carolina numbers in Heaven's accounting program, MicroSoul Redeemer, and the graphs rolled across the screen in heavenly gold on celestial black. The graphs showed a net decrease in Heavenbound souls, and a corresponding net increase in the Hellbound. God shook his head. "That's bad. Decidedly bad. Operation Tarheel initially gave us a four percent increase in net. Now we have an almost equivalent decrease."

God had been pleased, but not surprised, by the increase in the Heavenbound after Operation Tarheel kicked in. His subordinates had expressed shock and disbelief when He turned loose roughly fifty-eight thousand fallen angels, devils, demons, and assorted imps and gargoyles into North Carolina, with only the most lenient of rules to govern their behavior. It had been a great joke and an inspired operation, and Dayne Kuttner, the young mortal for whom he'd created the project, had responded magnificently. She'd torn Hell's second-in-command, a fallen angel named Agonostis, out of Lucifer's grip simply by loving him and making him love her.

Hell had no room for love.

Still, nearly everyone but God—in Heaven, on Earth, and in Hell—had been certain the whole state was on the fast track to damnation. Heaven's hosts expressed shock as redeemed devils and imps, recalled to Hell for straying from their appointed tasks, began applying at Heaven's gates for admittance; they watched in disbelief as damnedsouls looked at the events in North Carolina and found hope even in the midst of their Hellish torments—and repented.

But now God realized that somehow Lucifer had found an edge. North Carolina's numbers had reversed themselves, and the state's population of saved seemed to be heading downward at an alarming rate.

"The Father of Lies must have come up with a convincing one," God said. "I wonder what it is."

"Shall I form a task force to go down and investigate?"

Honorial had been itching to go to Earth ever since the Unchaining. God suspected he had friends among the Hellraised he wanted to visit, and that maybe he was a bit envious of the way things had turned out for Agonostis.

"No. No task force. I already told you, a physical presence by any of Heaven's forces is outside the bounds of my experiment . . . for now, in any case. No. Just monitor the situation for me, and when you find out what the unspeakables are up to, let me know."

Honorial nodded, disappointment clear in his expression. "You going to be around?"

"Page me. I have some work I need to take care of elsewhere."

God switched into her Goddess form on the run. She was going to have to hurry—those pagans could clean a buffet faster than a plague of locusts could wipe out a cornfield. If I'm lucky, God thought, hurrying back to Summerland, I'll get there before the ambrosia and the fried chicken run out.

Chapter 2

Dan Cooley jumped as a bolt of lightning slammed into a tree in the park nearby, momentarily lighting the predawn sky and casting the Raleigh street in eerie shades of blue and white. He mopped his face with a sweat-soaked sleeve and shifted on the vinyl car seat, trying to find a position that would let him drive without touching the seat with any portion of his anatomy. He felt his shirt sticking and tugging at his skin as he moved. Damned irritating. He tried the air conditioning again. Sometimes it worked, but not today.

North Carolina summers are the worst, he thought as he drove along the empty street. It's ninety out here already. Might break the one hundred mark by lunchtime . . . if it doesn't rain.

It probably would rain, though. The thunder and lightning had to be bringing rain with them sooner or later.

A sudden gust of wind blasted between two buildings and buffeted the car. Scraps of newspaper and assorted trash spiraled up from the gutter and skittered across his windshield. His headlights picked out several winos huddled against the stained brick of an abandoned building. One passed a brown paper bag to another. The third turned his face away as Dan drove by.

Eight months ago, this part of town hadn't been too

bad. It got worse every day, though. He passed Harriet's Fruit and Produce Company, which had still been in good shape when he moved to Raleigh. Broken bottles littered the empty parking lot. Someone had replaced the shattered glass panes with cardboard. Racist graffiti decorated the walls, along with crude drawings of nude women and oversized sexual organs and slogans like "Go to Hell for the Holidays."

The winos weren't the only bums living in the streets, though. Even some of the Hellraised were out of work. Dan saw stories about devils standing in bread lines and demons and gargoyles and imps clogging welfare offices demanding to be put on the rolls. According to some rumors, Hell was downsizing its operation in North Carolina because of the population drop as people fled the state.

God damn the Unchaining anyway. The state was driving straight to Hell, lights flashing all the way.

"I wish I could do something to make a difference," he muttered.

Lightning crashed into the top corner of the building at the next intersection and for an instant he saw the strobe-slowed images of bricks and trim flying in all directions. He hit his brakes to keep clear of debris. The rain started—a few hard, big splats on his windshield preceded a torrent so fierce that the roar of the rain drowned out the sound of the radio.

He slowed further and squinted past his flailing windshield wipers, looking for his turn.

There it was.

As he prepared to turn right, a small form dashed in front of him, momentarily illuminated by the glow of the headlights.

"Shit!" Dan slammed his foot on the brakes. The Mustang fishtailed on the wet road and slid to a stop.

"What the hell . . . ?"

A man raced behind the child. Both were sodden, tattered, bundled in filthy clothing. The rain blurred them, and they dashed out of his headlights before he could decide whether they were running toward something or away from it, but before he could move forward again, half a dozen young men ran after the pair, which answered the question. The young men hooted and yelled obscenities. Several threw bottles and pieces of brick.

He thought he heard one of them shout, "Get 'em! Get 'em!" and another yell, "Let's cut 'em!"; he couldn't be sure. The rain and the radio together made their voices tiny.

There were still no other cars on the road with him. Feeling uneasy, he backed up and aimed the headlights in the direction in which everyone had run.

The pack of teenagers was spread out in a semicircle, its prey trapped in the corner of a warehouse parking lot. Dan could make out baseball bats and broken bottles and a knife in the hands of the various attackers.

The voice of common sense told him, "You can't do anything; there are almost a dozen of them. Get to a phone fast and call the cops." He wished he had a car phone. That would have helped. He didn't, though. All he had was his car—with its doors locked against any intrusion from the dangerous world outside—and a conscience that he could tell wasn't going to let him flee to the nearest phone.

Dan felt his stomach knot. The thugs were closing in on the man and the kid. "Oh, screw it."

He yanked the gearshift, aimed the car at the middle of the gang, then floored the gas pedal. He jumped the curb; the impact rattled his teeth. As the tires hit the parking lot, chunks of gravel rang on the Mustang's chassis; he kept accelerating towards the group. He leaned on the horn the entire time.

It worked. The kids ran off, but not too far.

Dan skidded to a stop near the two figures. He reached over and unlocked the passenger door and yelled above the sound of the rain, "Get in!"

His overhead light wasn't working; the two of them couldn't see him, couldn't see that he didn't intend them any harm. He saw their dark forms move forward nervously, way too slow, and he yelled, "Hurry up, dammit! Those creeps aren't going to wait forever!"

The kid jumped into the darkness of the car. "In back!" Dan said, pushing him over the bucket seat.

The man yelped, then squeezed into the car and slammed the door. As he did, a rock banged off the hood.

"Shit!" Dan said. "Hold on!" He shifted into drive and peeled out of the parking lot. Something thumped against the trunk before they got completely away.

His heart didn't slow down for another minute. When the shakes passed, he said, "That was close! Oh, shit, that was close. Are you okay?" He tried not to notice the smell of the two of them, which approximated wet dog only if the dog in question had been roadkill for a couple of days.

The man mumbled something.

"Huh?" Dan asked.

"Got hit in the face by a rock. But, yeah, I'm fine."

"What about your kid?"

The man turned to stare at him. In the darkness, Dan only caught the outlines of his passenger, but he noticed something subtly wrong. His skin began to crawl.

"My kid?" the man asked. His acid-etched ground-glass voice held a note of bewilderment.

"Yeah." Dan glanced in the rearview mirror. He drove

beneath the light of a street lamp as he did, so he got a good look at the bright blue nightmare that popped over the back of the seat to grin at him. Heavy jowls hung in folds down both sides of its face, and beady black eyes stared out at him from a web of wrinkles. Dagger-pointed teeth poked out of the huge, lipless mouth, curving out and up toward the flat nose and down toward the receding chin. Two tiny horns erupted from the sloping forehead.

"Holy *shit*!" Dan stomped on the brakes. The car spun out of control. The Mustang spiraled to a halt in the empty intersection, then stalled.

Dan froze and pulled back from the thing. "What in God's name is that?"

"God had nothing to do with it. It's an imp."

Dan turned to look at the man beside him. His jaw dropped. Yellow eyes with square pupils stared back at him. Two horns larger than the imp's stuck out through holes in the ball cap, which bore the legend "George's Pepsi Vending Service." The devil's skin was covered with tiny shimmering copper scales.

"Jesus," Dan breathed.

The Hellraised monster grinned. "Nah, not hardly. I can understand though—folks get us confused all the time."

Dan felt dizzy. "Say what?"

"Oh nothing. I was just making a joke, you know?" The devil looked around. "I don't have a driver's license, but shouldn't we get out of the intersection? If I've learned one thing since I've been on Earth, it's that the yellow light means speed up."

Hell's monster had a point. Dan started the engine with difficulty, then continued down the street. "So he's an imp. And what—I mean, *who* are you?"

"My name's Puck. I'm a devil. Second class." The

tiny monster looking over Dan's shoulder whined. "That's Fetch. It's an imp. Class nine, level four. One level up from animated shit."

"Hello," Dan said to the imp. Jeez, he thought, it looks like a bright blue Shar Pei.

"Don't bother waiting for an answer. It can't talk. Too low on the pecking order," Puck said.

"All right. My name's Dan. Cooley." The stink, unbelievably, got worse. They were from Hell, and they smelled like it. He breathed shallowly and tried to think of a way to get them out of his car. "Why were those guys chasing you?"

"You know much about the Hellraised?"

"I know a few things. We haven't seen many of you *people* in Raleigh. Lot of you in Charlotte. Or so I've been told."

"Yeah. Used to be the case. Things were pretty good under Agonostis, and even Punksucker, the temp, wasn't too bad. I had a nice cubicle, a terminal, a Hellnet account, a demon crew. . . . The new boss is Hell, though, pardon my pun. Corporation policy's changed." The devil frowned. "Next thing I know, I'm waiting to be downsized—direct orders from the boss. Say you don't know much about our kind, huh?"

"No, that's not what I said."

"We can't hurt people. Those guys knew that. The imp and I were sleeping in a trash bin nobody was using; they found us there. Wanted to have some fun with a pack of cigarettes and some matches. Under different circumstances, it might have been cute. You know, like kids trying on grown-up clothes. They'll be in Hell before too long, might as well get their practice in here. Things being the way they are though, I didn't feel like playing. So we ran."

Dan's eyes watered from the stench. He considered the potential unpleasantness of torrential rain pouring into the car and weighed that against the stink, and rolled his window down. He knew they couldn't hurt him, but he'd also seen people who pissed off a demon or a gargoyle and had to deal with their ideas of revenge. They'd had a lot of experience in revenge. He didn't dare kick them out of his car, so he toughed out the stink. "I thought you guys could pop in and out at will. Why didn't you teleport away?"

"We can't."

"Why not?"

"It can't teleport without help," Puck said as he jerked his thumb at the imp. "Satan's flaming balls, man, it's lucky they gave it a hole to shit with. Wish I'd had one when I started out. Made life tough in my early days, let me tell you."

Dan felt queasy. "I see. So why didn't you vanish?"

The devil slouched. "I can't. Not anymore."

"I asked you before, why not?"

He sighed. "I've been fired."

"Say what?"

"Fired. You know, terminated. Pink-slipped. Booted out the back door. I already told you; the downsizing. Understand?" The devil scratched his crotch. "I've lost most of my powers, so I can't teleport or anything. You with me, genius?"

Dan clenched the steering wheel. "Look, lose the attitude. I just saved your asses, after all."

The devil's demeanor changed instantly. He cringed, moving as far away from Dan as he could. "Don't hurt me!" he wailed.

The imp squeaked and leaped to the floorboard. Dan looked over his seat. The tiny monster crouched as far away as it could. It looked at Dan and trembled.

"Oh, come on," Dan said, embarrassed. "It's okay. I'm not going to hurt you."

"You're lying!" Puck howled.

"No, I'm not." What's wrong with these two, he wondered.

"Honest?"

"Honest."

The devil's quivering subsided. "Well, okay." He straightened and managed a shaky grin. "Sorry about that. In Hell, you're either dominant or submissive; no in-between. I can't help it; after thousands of years, it's part of me. Didn't mean anything by it. Won't happen again, I promise."

Cold rain pounded Dan's left arm and the side of his face as he moved his hand to signal a turn. A small puddle had begun to form on the driver's side floorboard. "So where can I drop you off?"

The devil looked out the window. "I'm not sure," he said. "We was sleeping in that trash bin, but those guys know about it now. I'd rather not go back. Tell you what, just let us out right here."

"You sure? I could let you out somewhere else, if it isn't too far."

"Nah, thanks anyway." He looked puzzled for a moment. "That felt weird."

"What felt weird?"

"Haven't had a reason to say thanks to anybody for a long time. Just hit me kind of strange, you know?"

The rain fell harder. Dan glanced at the two Hellraised. They're what everyone's so scared of? Jesus, if I said "Boo!" right now, I bet they'd go through the roof.

"Why don't we do this," Dan said. "I'll let you out when I get to work. We have a lobby; you could hang out there until the rain slacks up."

"You have a job?" The devil acted as if Dan had said he was a millionaire. "What do you do?"

"I'm a DJ for a local radio station, WKTU. K-Rock Raleigh. Ever heard of it?"

"Afraid not. Of course, I don't get to listen to the radio much, since I don't own one." The devil shifted in the passenger seat. "You sure it'll be okay?"

"Probably."

"So what do you want in exchange?"

Dan shook his head. "I don't want anything. I know how hard it must be to have no place to sleep."

"And no money."

"That too." Dan glanced over at Puck. The devil huddled in his seat, head down, looking miserable. "You said you were fired?"

"Yep," Puck said. "See, we had an administrative shake-up just after we got here. Agonostis and Jezerael, two of the big bosses, got into a power struggle over the local branch of the Corporation. We small fry were running around like gremlins with our heads bitten off, trying to predict who would come out on top and sucking up to both sides just to be safe. I licked so many pairs of boots I wore my tongue smooth." He stuck it out for Dan's benefit. "Thee?"

"Very nice." Christ.

"So, of course nothing goes right. They both get busted, we get a temp, everybody relaxes a little, and then the new boss blows in—he's a Devil First Class, brevetted to Fallen Angel for this mission. He's gone as high as he can go in the company, and now he has to figure out a way to stay there, you know? Every other devil in the organization is gunning for him, so he decides to make an example and picks yours truly. Just my luck."

"Why you?"

The devil shrugged. "Why not? I suspect a certain

demon told him I wanted his job. And if I ever find out for sure . . ."

Dan pointed over his shoulder at the imp. "Is that what happened to what's-his-name?"

Puck snickered. "Fetch? No, that isn't what happened to it. That's rich—an imp involved in Company politics. Nah, all devils have imps; that's one of our few perks. The new guy took my old one, though, which pisses me off. I had it broken in just fine, and he decides he needs a midnight snack. No more imp. But right before I got the ax, the Company gave me this," he said with a nod to the back seat. "Sludge from the bottom of the barrel. Just adding insult to injury. The Fallen wipe their asses with class-nine imps. Deep-fried, the little bastards aren't too bad, but as for getting any useful work out of one . . ." He gave an exasperated sigh.

"So what have you been doing since you were fired?" Dan said, desperate to change the subject.

"Waiting."

"Waiting for what?" He pulled into the station's parking lot.

"To get recalled back to Hell." The devil shook his head slowly. "I don't have a job, but that doesn't mean I just go straight back. It takes transportation to get there . . . and the crosstown bus won't do. Not that I'm in any hurry to go home. Soon as I roll through the gates, I'll be busted back to gargoyle for certain. There're some demons with long memories smacking their lips at the thought; I just know it."

"How long have you been waiting to be summoned back?"

"Eight months? Yeah, eight months. That feels about right."

"You guys have only *been* here eight months. You've been waiting the whole time to be summoned back?"

"Ummm-hmmm. I have two theories. Either Scumslag, that's the new boss, forgot about me—and I'd love to think that was what happened—or my old enemy Roiling Pusbucket figured out some way to make it look like I intentionally delayed my return. I figure that's what's really going on. He's had it in for me for centuries." Puck shook his head. "I wish I'd thought of snitching on Roiling Pusbucket first. If I'd come up with an idea like that, I'd have made Devil First Class for sure."

Puck's self-pity and conniving vindictiveness appalled Dan, but the devil really did seem unhappy with his life. "Why don't you repent?" he asked. "I've heard that the Hellraised who repent get to go straight to Heaven."

The devil laughed, a harsh braying sound. "What a crock of shit. You think His Infernal Majesty would leave a loophole like that in the terms of our sentences? Please."

"You can't repent?"

"You have to regret what you've done, and mean it, to repent. And what do you think they do first thing when you get to Hell? They suck out all the memories of your sins, that's what. All of them. Schlooooop! One minute you're a sinner and the next minute all you can remember is your wife and kids and your friends and how good things were. Makes being in Hell rough, I tell you. At least until you find a place in the system. But it also makes it pretty damned difficult to repent. How am I supposed to repent what I don't remember?"

Good question, Dan thought. "I don't know." He pulled into his regular parking spot and turned off the ignition. Water splashed at his feet and soaked through his shoes and socks; he felt like he'd been for a swim in his clothing. But he didn't smell like Puck or Fetch, and neither would the Mustang, once they were out of it. "See that glass door? Head for it; I'll be right behind you."

He watched the two Hellraised shuffle to the building. They didn't even try to stay dry. Maybe from their perspective getting wet in a thundershower felt terrific. He locked the doors, rolled up the window, and ran past the devil and the imp into the station, trying to keep the few inches of him that were mostly dry from getting any wetter. Once inside, he looked for Roger; the security guard was nowhere in sight.

Puck and Fetch came cautiously into the lobby. Dan said, "There's coffee over there. Do you drink coffee?"

"Yeah. Thanks. Are we allowed to sit on the chairs and read the magazines?"

"Go ahead. The secretary will be coming in an hour from now, but you'll probably see the security guard before you see her. He's most likely in the restroom. He's an old guy with gray hair and a little bit of a limp. His name is Roger Petrie; just tell him I brought you in to wait out the storm."

"Okay," Puck said. Fetch had already poured both of them coffee from the coffee maker. He brought the cups over and silently handed one to Puck. The devil took it, thumped the imp on the head with one flicked finger, and told Dan, "See you around maybe, huh?"

Dan nodded and hurried away.

He stepped in front of the control booth's window and tapped on the glass. Sandy waved as he walked in. She held up a finger, indicating she would be with him when she finished, but kept right on talking into the mike. "—the song Bach would have written if he'd had an ounce of talent. Brought tears to my eyes, let me tell you. That was 'Trailer Park Madonna' by Rednecks In Paradise. And these Renaissance men have created a whole album of future masterpieces! The second number on our WKTU Two-fer-Tuesday is 'There's a Deer in My Headlights and a Gun in My Rack, But I Only Have Eyes for You,' coming at you from WKTU—K-Rock Ra-leeeeeigh!" She set the tape and switched off the mike. "Hiya, champ," she said. "How's it hanging?"

He grinned and flopped into a nearby seat. "Rednecks In Paradise?" He chuckled. "I thought Bernie nixed experimental Southern country crossover rock on the playlist."

"Fuck Bernie."

"Uh-oh. What happened this time?"

Sandy handed him a memo. "Word just came from his majesty's office. The A.M. and P.M. drives have to split the midday slot for now."

"What! Why?"

"Bernie fired Steve." Steve Gromman was the afternoon guy, and about the kindest, most easygoing human being Dan had ever known. "We have to cover his shift till they find a replacement. If they do."

"What do you mean, if?"

"Rumor has it that the owners are screaming for more cutbacks. Not only that, but I hear the sponsors are pissed off about the new rates. Doesn't help that our share has been going down for three months." She picked at a rip in her chair's vinyl upholstery. "To top everything else off, Darlene told me we lost the Chevrolet dealership to WRCK."

Darlene sold advertising for the radio, and she was efficient, funny, personable . . . and currently struggling to find something salable about WKTU. Dan frowned. "Wonderful. At this rate, Steve's going to have company at the unemployment office." He shook his head, frustrated. "Why'd Bernie fire him?"

"Don't know for sure. The old bastard caught him

sneaking in late and told him to step into his office. Next thing I know, Steve's clearing his stuff out."

Dan leaned back. "I covered for him once last week. He said Winnie caught the flu the baby had, and he stayed up all night taking care of them. I called him Monday about my eight-tracks and Winnie answered the phone. She still sounds terrible." Dan drummed his fingers on the arm of his chair. "Ever since Ted retired and Bernie took over, things have been going to shit around here."

"That isn't all the bad news."

Dan groaned. "What else?"

"You don't have a guest for your morning show."

"The Daltech rep canceled? Why?"

"Take a look." Sandy handed him a copy of the Raleigh *News and Observer*. "Front page, too."

Dan stared at the headline. DALTECH ANNOUNCES LAYOFFS. He skimmed the article beneath. The layoffs would begin in two weeks, and would eliminate thousands of jobs. He handed the paper back to Sandy, stunned. "No wonder he canceled. The sonuvabitch . . . I'd like to strangle him myself. Especially after that press release of his that guaranteed no downsizing this year."

Sandy dropped the newspaper to the floor. "Think your stepdad will get the ax, too?"

"He's not my stepfather, he's my mother's second husband." Dan sighed. "I have no idea. Maybe. He's been really tense lately, maybe he knew this was coming."

"So what are you going to do about your show?"

"Oh, Christ, I don't know. Cancel it, I guess. Just play the playlist."

"Too bad. That's right during peak driving time, too. Probably lose a bunch of listeners on their way to work."

"I know. Damn." Dan smiled. "Wait a minute! I've got an idea."

"Don't set any dangerous precedents."

"Thanks, smartass. I've got a guest waiting in the lounge. Hell, I've got two of them. No, wait, the imp can't talk."

Sandy stared at him. "What on Earth are you babbling about?"

"I ran into two Hellraised on the way to work this morning."

Sandy whistled. "Anybody get your license number?"

"No. I mean . . ." He laughed. "No. Look, just hang loose. I'll be back in a minute."

Dan strode down the hallway into the lounge and saw the security guard waving a makeshift cross at the two Hellspawn. "Go on, get!" Roger said to the Hellspawn.

"Rog, no! Wait a minute!" Dan yelled.

"It's all right, Mr. Cooley. I'm getting rid of them. They don't scare me!"

"I don't want you to get rid of them," he said. "Puck is my guest for the morning show."

"Huh?" The devil's eyes widened. "I'm what?"

"You're coming with me," Dan said as he took the devil's arm. "The control booth is this way. Where's the imp?"

Puck snapped his fingers and the imp darted to his side; it had been hiding in the plastic rubber plant. "He's right beside me."

"Good deal. Keep him there and hurry up."

The devil grinned. "There any money in this for me?"

"Money?" Dan looked at Puck's filthy clothes. "Yeah. We'll take up a collection after the show and scare up enough money for you to buy yourself some clean clothes. If you give me a good interview." He led the two Hellraised into the control room. Sandy's eyes widened. Then they widened further. Then she held her nose and started coughing.

"Sandy, this is Puck. Puck, this is Sandy." He pointed

at the imp, who clung to the devil's leg. "And that's Fetch. Right?"

Puck nodded. "Right."

Sandy seemed to have gotten past the initial shock of their stink and their presence. She still didn't seem pleased to meet them, though. Her smile was tight, her eyes glassy. "So you're a devil?"

The devil looked down the front of her loose blouse and leered. "That's right."

"Really? Well, I'm a lesbian. Pleased to meet you. Hang on a sec." Sandy turned back to the control panel and flipped her mike back on. "Guess what, folks—I am outta here. Gunga Dan's up next to take you to work with the interview from Hell. But before I go, I'm gonna leave you with an oldie from my own personal goddess, Melissa Etheridge. Remember—rock 'n' roll and cheap sex are the only things that separate us from the animals. This is the Iron Maiden of WKTU, K-Rock Raleigh, rockin' you into the day!"

"Sex separates us from the animals?" Dan said. "You don't hang out much on the Internet, do you?"

"Computers are an abomination. I'm from a family of Luddites; we still regard movable type with suspicion." Sandy got up and Dan found himself staring at the shift of her full breasts beneath her nubby raw-silk blouse. He sighed and focused on her face, which was beautiful even without makeup; serene and intelligent and always half-amused when she looked at him, as if she knew what he was thinking and didn't give a shit. She said, "Hey, want to drop by this Sunday? Julie and I are going to grill some dead animal flesh. Since it's a holy day, we'll tell the neighbors it's a burnt offering."

"Sounds promising," Dan replied as he slipped into place behind the control board. "I'll let you know. Mind if I bring a guest?"

Sandy raised an eyebrow. "You mean Meg?"

Dan put on the headset. "That a problem?"

"Meg's okay, I guess. I just don't feel like hearing about corporate depredations on the rain forest for two hours, or how bitterly treated we poor lesbians are, and how we need legislation to guarantee us especially *equal* equal treatment. She means well, but I can stand on my own two feet, thanks. I can make my way in the real world without needing somebody to shield me from the rough spots. I don't *need* the condescension."

"She doesn't mean to be condescending. Her uncle's gay, and I guess the world isn't especially warm and fuzzy toward gay Republican bankers—she feels a real burning desire to do something that will help."

"Great. She needs to find a cause besides mine. Anyway, Oprah was right. Excellence is its own defense against prejudice. If you're good enough, the world will make room."

Dan nodded and aimed the conversation back to the weekend. "So no Meg. I could bring *Janna*." He grinned at her. "But then could I trust you?"

"Me? Prefer a tall gorgeous blonde over a short plump brunette? What do you take me for?" She laughed. "Sure. Bring Janna. Maybe if you're lucky she'll be able to keep her hands off me. Later." She winked at him and sauntered out of the booth, her hips swinging in a gesture of flagrant seduction. She knew Dan thought she was attractive—that he would have been interested in her had she been available—and sometimes she couldn't resist a little taunting.

"Nice piece of ass," Puck remarked.

"Oh, yeah. Ass, tits, face . . ." Dan set up his CDs. "Nice piece of brain, too. Song's about through. I have to do the six A.M. news and an hour's worth of music and chat. We do the interview at seven. Just sit back and relax. Oh. When I finally get to the interview, remember, we have an eight-second delay, but even so, I don't want to have to use the bleeper after every third word, so no obscenities. Understand?"

Puck nodded. Dan could have sworn the devil looked a little nervous, but he decided it was probably a trick of the light. "All right. Here I go."

He switched on the mike as Melissa finished off the last notes of "Talking to My Angel." His voice metamorphosed into its deeper, fuller announcer mode. "Turn *off* those alarms, put out the cat and the mistress, and let's *go*! You're rockin' with Gunga Dan and WKTU—K-Rock Raleigh; the howling hordes of ninety-six point three are on their way to your house; and IIIIITTT'S MORRRRRNNNNNNIINNG!

"This just in. The North Carolina State Legislature passed a bill yesterday declaring toy poodles to be an endangered species. Since the Unchaining, these cuddly canines' numbers have decreased as the Hellraised attempt to resolve that age-old controversy: 'Tastes Great!' or 'Less Filling!' The bill was later amended to include Pomeranians, Yorkies and Corgis. A proposal to extend endangered status to the Mexican Chihuahua was overwhelmingly defeated, however. Said one senator, 'We had to draw the line somewhere.' " He punched up the klaxon, let it sound for a second, then moved into his next bit.

"News flash! A small riot erupted last night in the parking lot of the Church of Jesus Christ American. According to witnesses, the weekly burning of rock albums and classic novels was disrupted when a demon leaped out of the bonfire and cried 'More Fabio!' "

Dan played the "mob screaming" sound effect, the one that ended with a Bronx cheer. He did a few more stories, mostly centered around the Hellraised, played a few songs, ran the advertisements, did his top-ten list of things to do in Raleigh, joked on the air with Marilyn, the DJ who did the real news, played some more music.

While Marilyn did the seven A.M. news, he turned to Puck. "You're up next. You don't have to be funny. If you are funny, that's great, but if you aren't funny, I can be funny for both of us. All you have to do is answer my questions. You ready?"

Puck nodded.

Dan cut from the ads to the set piece he and Sandy had worked up to open the interviews, Fleetwood Mac's "Tell Me Lies" with voice-overs of Richard Nixon saying "I am not a crook" and a soundbite from the O.J. Simpson trial and George Bush's infamous "Read my lips" quote and Hillary Clinton saying she did nothing illegal in the Whitewater fiasco. When it finished rolling, Dan hit his intro hard.

"What can I say about my guest this morning? He's here! He's bad! He's the Guest . . . from . . . Hell! Want to know if Aunt Marge took your suggestion and headed South when she punched her ticket? Want to know if your boss really is the Spawn of Satan? Want to know if anyone knows about you and that hot little number in Accounting? Then get on the phones and ask, because this morning you're gonna get answers. Our guest comes to us straight from a tour of the six hundred and sixty-six levels of the Abyss, and boy are his wings tired! I present to you the famous, the IN-famous, Puck!"

Dan grinned at the devil. "So tell me, Puck—according to you, you're one hot dude from Hell. You been there, done that, bought the T-shirt. So . . . what gives with reruns?"

The devil blinked at Dan in confusion. "Reruns?"

"Oh, come on. Don't play coy with me! Ever since

the Unchaining I've got *Full House* on my TV set five times a week, and twice on Saturdays! You don't expect me to believe it's because people are actually watching it, do you? And what about infomercials? *Wheel of Fortune*? What about *The Montel Williams Show*? Do you expect me to believe it's all a coincidence?"

Puck shifted in his seat. "Well, no, but . . ."

"Yeah, yeah, we've heard it all before. 'Herr Judge, ve ver just following orders!' Speaking of which, how's Hitler doing?"

"Who?"

"Hitler? Adolph? You know, the short dumpy dark-haired guy who believed in the racial superiority of tall muscular blondes?"

The devil blinked in confusion. "Sorry, I didn't work in Personnel."

"Here we go again! Oh well, forget Hitler. Give us the inside scoop on the Big Man himself, okay?"

"The big man?"

"The Prince of Darkness! Lord of the Hoary Nether-worlds! Satan!"

Puck shivered. "What about Him?"

"Well, just between you, me, and the wall, is he really the epitome and sum of evil itself? Or is it all just a front?"

"A front?"

"Hey, you can tell me! All public figures have at least two personalities; one to trot out for the troops and the real McCoy. So what's he actually like? Is he the ultimate badass like they say? Or is he secretly a shy kind of guy? You know, listens to Michael Bolton and cries when the hunters shoot Bambi's mother? Fuzzy slippers and warm milk at bedtime?"

The devil stared at Dan as though he were insane. "I—don't think so."

"I guess you're right. Probably feels like he's got to live up to the rep. So enough about Satan. What about you? You're unemployed at the moment, is that right?"

"Well, yes. Unfortunately."

"Hey—maybe we can help you find a job! Best to go with what you know, right? So tell me Puck, what'd you do in Hell?"

"Do?"

"Your occupation in Hell. What was it? Chief torturer? Convenience store manager? Wastewater treatment plant operator?"

The devil wiped a hand across his forehead. Dan pantomimed taking a deep breath and letting it out. Puck imitated him. "Nah, nothing glamorous like that. I changed jobs a lot, mostly within the bureaucracy. Last position I had was Employee Relations and Morale Clerk. I translated company directives from up above into unintelligible corporate-speak for the floor workers."

"What happened?"

Puck looked like he was relaxing a little. "I'm not sure. Upper management said they were engaging in a reevaluation of my long-term prospects for maximizing opportunity situations, and that they had unilaterally reprioritized my infrastructural imperatives pending lateral corporate placement by transfer to a positive-image-minimized employment situation with a sum-negative advancement track and a corporately advantageous payment structure."

Startled, Dan laughed. "They said *that*?"

"They said that."

"Oooooo—sounds like Hell."

"Yeah, well." The devil raised his eyebrows and shrugged. "We have to expect things like that. A lot of middle management flows our way."

Dan laughed again. "You know, I always suspected

that. Even radio stations have middle managers." The devil was turning out to be a decent guest after all. He stank, but he didn't stink. At least their share wouldn't drop because of him. In the back of Dan's mind, an idea began to form.

"So tell me, where do you see yourself in five years, Puck?"

He only half-listened to the answer. His plan took shape. It was outrageous. Implausible. Incorrigible. Audacious. It would make that bastard Bernie yank out what was left of his hair.

It was perfect.

The devil stopped to catch his breath, and Dan waved him to silence. "Puck," he said, "repeat after me. 'The rain in Spain falls mainly on the plain.' " He did it with a faux-British accent.

"The rain in Spain falls mainly on the plain." The devil mimicked his delivery and his accent, then asked, "Why did you want to me to say that?"

Dan leaned forward. "Ever heard of George Bernard Shaw? *Pygmalion*? *My Fair Lady*?"

"No."

"You will." Dan focused on his microphone. "Listen up, Raleigh. Puck's an unemployed devil—a social leech with no job and no place to live, and he hasn't had a bath since Noah floated out of the Flood. In fact, he reminds me of an uncle on my mother's side. I say we turn him into an upstanding North Carolinian. We'll scrub him down, dress him up, and make a new man of him. If we can shape him up, we can shape any of them up. We'll call it the Great Devil Makeover. Grab a phone and let me know what you think! Call me now!"

Dan cued up "Sympathy for the Devil" by the Rolling Stones and flipped off his mike.

Puck watched him, those yellow eyes disconcertingly excited.

"You like it?" Dan asked.

"I like it," Puck said. "If there's a steady paycheck in it, I'll believe anything you say."

"*Ghostbusters*, right?" Dan said, catching the line. He didn't let the devil's sudden enthusiasm bother him. He smiled. "I'm going to put this station back in the black, my fine fiend. And you're going to help me."

Chapter 3

The treadmill increased its speed again and Janna English moved from an easy lope into an outright run. Her feet pounded on the moving surface, her body gleamed golden beneath the gym lights, and sweat slicked her skin and made her glow. She checked her form in both the front and side mirrors. Shoulders up. Head erect. Knees up. Arms loose. Her hair, swept back in a loose ponytail, stuck to her neck in places. Irritating.

I will get the part, she told herself. I will be the best actress to audition. The director and producer will see me as the main character, they will have seen my work in *Blackout* and they will be impressed. They will want me. They will want me.

Paul from Building C stepped into the main gym from the sauna, wearing a towel around his waist. He was close to forty, with thin legs and ugly feet. He was a pathetically unimaginative lover, too, but he did have his strong points. She smiled at him.

He leaned against the mirror right in front of her, which prevented her from checking her forward form, and smiled back at her.

"Hi, babe. Want to go back to the apartment and screw before I go to work? My friend and I miss you."

He pulled the towel aside to show her how much he missed her.

"I wouldn't do that if I were you," she said, maintaining her pace. "Management monitors the gym. And I can't come back with you. I'm working out." She needed to not lose her temper with him. He had a ridiculous amount of money in his bank account, and she was short enough on funds that some of it would come in useful, if they could stay friends. Or if she could maintain polite relations with his "friend." "I'm up for a part today, so I have to get this out of the way now."

"Cattle call?"

"Callback. Reading." She tried to project her certainty that she would get the part. "My agent said they were very enthusiastic when they called her to set up the time."

"Oh." He watched her.

She thought, Would you move your ass out of my way so I can see what I'm doing? She didn't say anything.

He looked at the clock behind her. "I'm running out of time."

"Don't let me keep you. I have to lift weights after this, and today is an upper body day—that takes longer."

He looked disappointed. Naturally. She smiled at him to lessen the sting, and he said, "Well, I guess I'll be going, then. You want to get together tonight?"

"Can't," she said. "I have a shoot for a local department store catalog tomorrow morning—early. If I don't get my sleep, my eyes will be puffy." He could say he was dating an actress. She didn't see any reason why he needed to say he was going steady with one.

"You doing okay for money?"

"No. I will be. If the movie comes through."

He smiled a little. "In the meantime, why don't you let me help you out?"

She smiled again. "When I make my million, I'll pay you back in style."

He turned to leave, and she called after him, "Turn on the radio for me, would you? Ninety-three point six. It helps to have something to listen to while I work out."

He nodded, turned on the radio, and left. When she got back to her apartment, she'd find a thousand dollars on the kitchen counter. Cash. No need to report it, no need to bank it—all she had to do was spend it. One of the nice little dividends to having a few movies in her past; now more than ever, men wanted to be with her, and they liked to give her gifts so she'd want to keep spending time with them.

She listened to another of her boyfriends doing his morning show. Dan wasn't one of the money boyfriends. He was one of the public appearance boyfriends. He was a celebrity in his own right, which gave him legitimacy, but he wasn't as well known as she was, so he didn't outshine her. He had a good body and a photogenic face, and he was the requisite two inches taller than her when she was wearing heels, so that they didn't look ridiculous in photographs. She couldn't afford to look ridiculous. The North Carolina celebrity scene didn't have the size or scope of that in New York or Hollywood. A few bad photos here could cost her work.

He was talking to a devil.

That was a first, even for him. The devil discussed what he hoped he would be doing in five years, Dan made an abrupt transition to quoting *My Fair Lady*, and all of a sudden he had her complete attention. She slowed the treadmill to a walk, manually overriding the variable-intensity program she'd chosen; she wanted to be able to hear what he was saying.

"Listen up, Raleigh. Puck's an unemployed devil—a social leech with no job and no place to live . . ." She continued her cool down walk while Dan presented his Great Devil Makeover idea to Raleigh's morning commuters. "Grab a phone and let me know what you think! Call me now!"

Her instincts told her this was an opportunity. It didn't seem like much on the surface, but everything about the Hellraised could command national, and sometimes even international, attention.

She suspected that Dan was about to find himself in the spotlight. She decided she'd like a large portion of that attention for herself. She resolved to call Dan and offer her support—maybe she could suggest herself in the role of acting coach. Or maybe she could just be there, getting her picture taken. NORTH CAROLINA ACTRESS REDEEMS HELLRAISED. She could see the headline. And the subhead, too. "Will Play Herself in Major Motion Picture."

Chapter 4

Meg Lerner rolled over and yawned. Seven A.M. and her alarm clock gave her not the voice of Dan, the man she thought she might be falling in love with, but the voice of Marilyn, his morning show sidekick, doing the news. She stretched but didn't get up. She wanted to hear the interview, which always came on at seven. Dan had announced the day before that a representative from Daltech, the big Research Triangle Park electronics firm, was going to be his morning interview. Considering that Daltech was one of the biggest employers left after the post-Hellraising exodus began, Meg was more than a little interested to hear what the man had to say.

But the Daltech rep wasn't there. Instead, Dan started interviewing a devil. He kept the tone light, and Meg thought some of the stuff on both sides turned out pretty funny, but it wasn't what she'd wanted to hear.

That is, it wasn't until Dan suggested doing a Great Devil Makeover and rehabilitating the devil.

That idea interested Meg a lot.

Meg spent a bit of time on the Internet when she wasn't trying to keep her little law practice afloat or trying to figure out where she and Dan stood with each other. And online, she'd been reading some disturbing things. Being a North Carolina native, and one who'd determined to stay come Hell or high water—or just high water, since Hell had already arrived—she'd closely watched the posts in the alt.hellraised newsgroups.

Recently, some of the posts had been getting extreme. Along with the usual wackos, flamers, and kids who were just trying to prod a response out of someone, a dark undercurrent of violence had begun to build. One guy from out west someplace was, in all seriousness, trying to encourage foreign governments to "Do The Decent Thing" and drop a few nukes on North Carolina since Washington didn't have the balls. A lot of outsiders blamed the state for its sudden population of Hellraised, and wanted to impose measures restricting everything from sex to free speech in the state in an attempt to make it pure enough that God would send the Hellraised home. No one seemed to think that North Carolinians were up to handling the problem on their own.

Meg did. She thought that North Carolina, with its historic tenacity and determination, might even manage to make something positive out of its Hellish invasion.

And there was Dan, offering the perfect proposal to a beleaguered state.

Meg sat up in the bed, thoughtful. She listened for a while to the tenor of the calls he was receiving, counting the number of people who just wanted to swear at him and comparing that to the number of people who thought maybe he was onto something.

The response, mostly positive, surprised her. North Carolinians had already discovered they couldn't run the Hellraised off their land. Killing them didn't work—the bodies just reappeared and the killer got stuck with an enormous bill sent straight from Hell for the damages. But as far as Meg knew, no one had ever tried to make the Hellraised into something North Carolina could live with.

Maybe it was time to try.

Chapter 5

At ten, Dan left Marilyn with the news and instructions to play music until he got back, and answered the urgent summons he'd gotten from the station manager's office an hour earlier. He rapped on the door and leaned in, being sure when he did to keep his face serious. "You wanted to see me, Bernie?"

"Damned right. Sit down." Bernie Hatcher, fortyish, pasty-faced, with thinning hair and a thickening middle, fussed with a spoon and a bottle of Pepto Bismol, then dropped the spoon and drank the medicine straight from the bottle. He wiped his mouth and turned his phone around. "Do you see this?"

Dan looked at the flashing extension lights. "Yes?"

"Do you have any idea what kind of chaos that little announcement of yours has caused? Darlene says she's logged over two hundred calls so far. And . . ." Bernie paused. "Who's manning the booth?"

"Marilyn. She's doing the news now, and if she needs to, she'll put music on for me when she's done. What's the matter?"

"What's the matter? You hear that, God? He wants to know what's the matter. This schmuck can't figure it out on his own." Bernie liked to talk to God. Dan hoped God would answer some time real soon—he figured if he did, the station would have one less Bernie and he'd have one less headache. "This!" Bernie yelled. "This is the matter!" He picked up the phone and slammed it on the desk.

Dan stared at Bernie and smiled cheerfully. He wanted to kill the little tyrant—one of his best friends was unemployed with a sick wife and an infant child because this man had a fetish for time clocks. But killing him wouldn't solve Dan's problems, and getting WKTU back on track would. If the station started doing well, maybe Dan could force Bernie to give Steve Gromman his job back.

"Bernie," he said. "Telephone calls are a *good* thing. We *want* phone calls. We *like* them. Phone calls mean we got people's attention, made them listen, forced them to do more than sit on their cans passively sucking in sound waves. It doesn't matter if we made them mad. We made them *care*. That matters. The Great Devil Makeover is going to make a lot of people care. And in the process, it's going to put us in the black and on top of the ratings."

Bernie leaned back and glared. "I'm listening."

"The Unchaining is the biggest thing in this state, in this country. Hell, maybe even the entire world. People are fascinated and obsessed and burning with curiosity about the Hellraised. Hell's little devils cause a lot of trouble, but when it comes right down to it, we really don't know much about them. That's going to change, though. Now we've got a devil who's willing to talk and who has a reason to want to change—and think about what heroes we'll be if we can change him. If we can turn Puck into a good guy, Bernie, you will be a god, man."

Bernie didn't look convinced.

Dan kept going. "The people of this town will be kissing your ass and begging to buy spots on this station.

In the beginning of course a few people are going to be upset, but even the ones who are upset are going to listen and they're gonna talk. The only bad publicity is no publicity."

"Uh-huh. But what about the sponsors? You can bet your ass that, even as we speak, religious wackos all over this city are calling every business that advertises with us to demand a boycott."

"You may be right. But we'll still keep the sponsors; in fact, we'll be turning new ones away for lack of air time."

"How do you figure that?"

"First, if those folks called, they must have been listening. And they're going to listen even more in the days to come. I plan to get the sponsors involved in the whole makeover process. Get them out there in front of people saying, 'Yes, we support WKTU. Yes, we want to make a difference, and we're doing something to make our state a better place to live. We may be doing it one devil at a time, but by God we're doing it.' "

Dan wished he had an American flag blowing in the breeze behind him right then. Maybe someone to play "The Star-Spangled Banner" softly in the background. He said, "This is the American thing to do, Bernie. The patriotic thing. We see a problem. We take a stand. And then we go to work, filling those sandbags, feeding those hungry children . . . and bringing those Hellraised devils and demons and fallen angels into the fold. We make a *difference*."

He could see the glitter of unshed tears shining in Bernie's eyes, or maybe it was the glitter of newborn greed.

He said, "Plus, by getting the sponsors involved, we move the cost for the entire project onto their shoulders."

"Great. It doesn't cost us anything, it gets us listeners, it gets us sponsors." Bernie nodded. "But what if he screws up? What if he can't be rehabilitated?"

"No, Bernie. Wrong question. We aren't selling a sure thing here. I know that. Our listeners are going to know that. He probably can't be turned around. But we are selling hope, and hope has been pretty hard to come by. The question isn't 'What if he can't be rehabilitated?' It's 'What if he can?' "

The station manager leaned forward and rested his elbows on his desk. "So what if he can be changed? We're talking one lousy devil."

"No. We're talking the entire state of North Carolina suddenly out from under this cloud. We're talking a problem that can be fixed, not a curse from God. We're talking the end of the exodus, people moving back, the return of life as we knew it. Think about it, Bernie. Hell of a thing to accomplish, isn't it?"

"Okay, Dan, I'll tell you what. We'll go forward on this, but only provisionally. If it looks like things aren't going well, we can always back out and claim Puck is beyond help."

"Even if it's not true?"

"We do it on that basis, or none at all."

Dan clenched his fist. Ted Argent, the old station manager, would have seen the possibilities in an idea like this. Bernie was only interested in a sure thing, and a quick cover for his ass if necessary.

But that was all right. He could work within those boundaries. In talking to Bernie, in trying to sell him on the project, Dan had totally sold himself. Now he wanted to do this. He wanted to make the project work not just to get ratings, but because he realized every word of what he'd said to Bernie had been true. A radio promotion, a stupid gag to get people to listen to the station, might actually be enough to make a difference in the state he'd chosen to call home. And if Bernie couldn't see the real payoff at the end of the project, it didn't matter. Dan could see it, and Dan was the one who was going to make it come true.

He put out his hand. "All right, Bernie. We'll do it your way."

The station manager nodded and gave Dan's hand a weak, damp clench. "Good. Keep me informed."

Chapter 6

Lucifer sat at the head of the boardroom table with a bag of deep-fried damnedsouls and a few sulphur-cured imps on sticks tucked away in case the meeting ran long. Tracking gave a brief report on the Hellraised who'd gone AWOL upon reaching North Carolina. The tracking team was actually doing a good job, but since they hadn't found all of the missing Hellraised, Lucifer ripped the head off of the department manager and threw him into the Pit, then promoted the first assistant to her place. Decisive management, he thought.

He listened through the department head of Research and Development's long-winded report on the progress he was making on digitally controlled torture devices. At another time Lucifer might have found the report fascinating, and really the color overhead projections of pie graphs and bar graphs of inflicted pain with old methods versus inflicted pain with new methods were very nicely done. Lucifer experienced a momentary surge of interest when R&D brought in a couple of damnedsouls for the demo.

But Scumslag was down from his away mission in North Carolina to give the half-year report on the progress of Satco, that tiny little division of Netherlands Industries that had garnered such a lot of enthusiasm from everyone in the main branch of the company. Lucifer wanted to hear what Scumslag had to say, and not even an amusing demonstration of R&D's new toys seemed like much of a diversion while he was waiting.

Communicable Diseases was next on the agenda, but when R&D sat down, Lucifer pointed to Scumslag. "You next," he said.

Scumslag smiled. "My thanks, Your Magnificent Awfulness. I'll keep this brief. Our statewide net in damnedsouls is up four percent, statewide morale—as measured by our twenty-point morale index—is falling at half a percentage point per month, murder and suicide rates are rising, and the altruism index is way down. Plus, we show a financial profit in this second quarter of forty-seven-point-five-three million dollars. Net."

The devil, the only one in the boardroom who wasn't a fallen angel or snack food, grinned around the table at the other department heads.

"That's a good start," Lucifer said. "But how is the Devil's Point project coming?"

Devil's Point had been the idea of the first CEO of Satco, Agonostis, before he went over to the other side. It was to be an amusement park built in North Carolina, offering one-of-a-kind amusements for a slightly less-than-average day rate. It was to have a water park with real mermaids; a zoological park with living specimens of extinct creatures from every one of Earth's geological eras; a library with every book that had ever been written in every language that had ever been spoken; a live-action role-playing game park with special effects from Hell; the ultimate mall, that offered every product the mind could imagine; body shops where the customer could buy the body he or she had always wanted; and much, much more.

The customer would be able to find almost exactly what he wanted at a competitive cost. Hell would make a nice profit on that, because it had virtually no manufacturing costs. And when the customer knew *exactly* what he wanted, he would find, instead of another shop or attraction, a magical door. That door would take him to a secret, hidden part of the park. Desire's Point. Where he could have exactly what he most desired.

For a slightly higher price.

The park looked tremendous on the drawing board. Unfortunately, it hadn't gotten past that stage yet. "Everything is ready to go," Scumslag said. "We've located the land we want in Pender County, right next to Topsail Beach. We've found a hundred square miles that we can buy up relatively cheap—land prices have fallen through the floor since we arrived. The only problem right now is that no one will sell us the land, and we're hampered by His rules about humans knowing whom they're dealing with."

"I don't recall much resistance from humans when it comes to dealing with the devil," Lucifer said. "They've always been greedy little bastards."

"Yes, they have. But this particular block of land happens to have fallen into the hands of people who aren't motivated by greed."

"Fundamentalists?" Lucifer scoffed. "They can be tempted."

"Oh, no, Your Horribleness. Much worse than Fundamentalists. *Environ*mentalists."

The fallen angels around the table hissed, and even Lucifer made the sign of the evil eye. "Find another piece of land," Lucifer said. "You'll never get their nasty little claws out of that one."

"But I think I will." Scumslag's smile grew huge. "Greed won't get them, but I think their politically correct agenda will. More than anything else, they want the power to force other people to do things their way or no way at all. So I'm working on that angle. I'll get 'em."

Chapter 7

The number 4 blinked at Dan from the answering machine as he walked into his apartment. He increased the speaker volume, punched play, then went into the kitchen for a Coke.

Beep!

"Dan, this is Darlene. I've been calling our sponsors. A lot of them are holding back on a commitment, but I've got some names for the ones who want to participate in the Makeover. Bernie says this is your baby and your vision, so you'll have to talk to them on your day off. He wants you to handle it personally. Sorry. Bye."

My day off, Dan thought. Well, it was my idea.

Beep!

"Hello, machine. I have a son who winds your tape on occasion. Please tell him I love him and would appreciate hearing from him before summer's end. Thank you, Mr. Machine."

Dan grinned. "All right, Mom," he told the empty room, "I'll drop by this afternoon."

Beep!

"Hi baby! It's Janna. I heard your show, and your Great Devil Makeover idea sounds wonderful! In fact, I'd like to volunteer my expertise. I can teach him how to walk and speak and use proper etiquette and be charming at boring functions and wear a suit and tie a tie . . ." She laughed. "And I won't even charge him for all this valuable wisdom. I'd love to see you, and I'm available this evening, so if you want to bring your devil by for his first lesson, give me a call and confirm. Thinking of you! Bye!"

Beep!

"Dan, it's Meg. Listen, I think you're onto something here. I have an idea about this makeover thing of yours that I'd like to bounce off you. Call me. Bye."

Dan leaned against the wall, thoughtful. He liked both women a lot. Meg seemed a little more *real*, but Janna reminded him so much of Francie sometimes that it made his breath catch in the back of his throat. Both of them hinted from time to time that they would like to spend more time with him. They didn't know about each other, and he doubted either would be thrilled to discover he was dating the other. Not that any commitments had been asked for or given. Still, he probably ought to choose one and break off with the other.

Easy to say. But which one?

Dan turned on the stereo and settled on the couch. He stared at the ceiling.

What should he do? Was there a right thing? Did he need to do anything? After all, it wasn't as though any of them had made any demands. And if he broke up with either, it would mean he was ready to get more serious about the other. He wasn't.

He wondered briefly if either woman was seeing anyone else. He didn't think so. Janna teased him about her "stable." She didn't sound serious, so she was probably just kidding. But maybe not . . .

And Meg made the sign of the cross at issues of *Modern Bride* and said she carried a silver bullet to ward off bridesmaids. But was she really so anti-marriage? Or was she just testing his reactions?

He took a swallow of Coke.

Neither one of them was Francie.

He looked at the Coke, wishing for just an instant that it was something harder . . . but he didn't do that anymore. He'd giving up trying to drown his sorrows. He'd discovered his sorrows swam a hell of a lot better than he did. This time he managed to keep himself from digging out the old photo albums, though, or pulling out the wedding picture that until he'd moved back to North Carolina had sat atop his desk. He was, he thought, getting stronger.

Cancer had not been kind to Francie, and he had a hard time remembering her as the girl he loved in high school, the young woman who married him when he had nothing in the world to offer her, the friend who played roller hockey in the driveway with him and didn't mind getting hit by the ball. All of that got lost in the memories of that last year, with Francie pale and bald from radiation, thin and frail and waif-eyed and bruised from the chemo and the IVs. In the end, little of Francie remained. Pain ate the laughter and devoured the joy and left her crumpled in the hospital bed, broken and defeated. He loved her—he offered God anything to take the cancer away from her, to let her be herself again—but in the end, Dan had been helpless to do anything but watch as she slipped away.

He sipped the Coke.

Francie had been his gift from Heaven. He'd had her. He'd loved her. He'd lost her. He'd learned that every love had a beginning and an ending, and the more love there was in the beginning, the more the ending hurt.

So he had devised a simple expedient for preventing any more of that anguish. He wouldn't fall in love ever again.

Chapter 8

The biggest reason Dan had been willing to move away from KWDY in Boulder to take the morning slot at a smaller radio station in Raleigh was the chance to be close to his family again. He'd been the local-boy-made-good when he came back. Ted had given him free rein with the morning content, including an unprecedented freedom with the playlist. Then Ted, in the manner of all people everywhere who were smart, fun to work with, and talented, had received a whopping offer for a better job from a major market station and had flown happily away, leaving Bernie, that human pile of bat guano, in his place.

Dan, on the other hand, had decided to stay.

He glanced at the rearview mirror to check his hair, wondering if it had gotten long enough that his mother was going to give him a hard time about it. He checked the time—4:45 P.M. If he were lucky, he could visit with his mom and get out the door before Arthur came home.

Arthur.

Dan made a face. Arthur, the all-around great guy; Arthur, his mother's hero; Arthur, the big twenty-five-year man at Daltech; the guy in upper management who "took her away from all of that," and into a big house and fancy lifestyle. Now Arthur-the-Savior was as likely as anyone to be facing the ax, and the family was going to see how steadfast he was. Dan feared old Art would split, and his mother would get her heart broken again. And end up owing a lot of money she couldn't afford to pay.

The steady, cold rain, still pouring down out of a bleak gray sky, had left a puddle the size of Lake Michigan across her driveway. Dan decided to park in the street rather than try to figure out a way to get out of the car without getting his feet soaked.

He stepped onto the brick porch. Something new hung from one of the white columns—a small plaque. He read it and frowned.

WELCOME TO THE HOME
OF ARTHUR AND PATRICIA HILL

"Hi Mom," he said as the door opened.

"Well, hello stranger," his mother said and hugged him. "Come on in. Watch Arthur's plant."

Dan returned the embrace, then moved past her into the house. "I can't stay long. I have to work on a pitch for the new promotion I'm doing for the station."

She gave him one of those long, omniscient mother looks she'd perfected back when he was fourteen and smuggling *Playboy* magazines into his room to hide between the mattress and the box springs. "I heard your show this morning."

"Great idea, don't you think?"

Still that look, but now with the raised eyebrow, too. The raised eyebrow indicated her opinion that he'd taken a definite slip into the realms of the sanity-challenged.

"You don't think, huh?"

She dropped into her La-Z-Boy recliner and leaned back. She shook her head slowly, and finally said, "I think a great deal about a great many things. I'd like to see some evidence that you do. What *possessed* you, Daniel? Or maybe that's the answer as well as the question. Maybe it was demonic possession. Or temporary insanity."

"Why? Come on, Mom—this is an incredible opportunity."

"Yes, it is . . . to help the Hellspawn that are causing the ruin of North Carolina. To give work to one of the monsters responsible for your dad being on the brink of losing his job. I'm afraid I don't see the opportunity in that."

"First, Arthur isn't my dad. He's the man you married, and I'm happy that you found someone you love, but *my* dad is that jerk out in Topeka who left us." His mother stiffened, and Dan, for just an instant, wished he'd let the "dad" thing slip for once.

"Cynthia calls him 'Dad.' "

"Cynthia was nine when you married him. I was thirteen. That makes a difference. And I didn't intend to talk about Arthur. I intended to talk about his job. If we can get industries to move back here, to realize that North Carolina is still a good place to be, then Arthur *won't* lose his job. And neither will a lot of other good people. *That* is what I'm trying to make happen."

"You can't change the Hellraised. They went to Hell because they were evil. Because nobody could change them. And now they're here in North Carolina, doing their evil, and they are going to be here until the last person leaves the state. I'll tell you, Daniel, if we could sell the house in this market, Arthur and I would move. But in eight months the valuation on our home has dropped from one hundred twenty thousand dollars to thirty thousand dollars, and it will probably drop further. Even if we could find a buyer, we couldn't afford to sell."

"I'm sorry." Dan leaned forward. "I know things are hard for you—for everyone. That's why I'm trying to make them better."

"This isn't the way to do it. A panel of experts on Oprah all agreed that they can't be redeemed."

The Oprah defense. Dan had gotten this one before. "Who were these experts?"

"Theologians and evangelists. They were there for a show called 'Which Church Is God's Real Church?' They didn't agree on much else, but they agreed on that."

"What experience did they have with the Hellraised, Mom?"

His mother looked annoyed. "They're . . . theologians . . . and . . . evangelists." The clipped voice snapped with irritation. "They've spent their entire adult lives studying things like this."

"Are they from North Carolina? Have they dealt with the Hellraised?"

"They deal with God."

"That nurse Dayne Kuttner dealt with God. He listened to her. You show me proof that He listens to the pompadoured Jesus-shouters whose big cry is that God needs more money. You prove to me that He listens to the theologians who believe dogma and doctrine are more important than caring for people who need help. Prove to me that God agrees with them. And when you prove that, I'll listen to what those snake-oil salesmen and hate mongers have to say about our problems."

His mother sighed and shook her head. "You were a pain in the neck when you were little, too. You never could believe someone other than you might be right." She put the recliner's footrest down and leaned forward. "I'll give you credit for having good intentions, Dan. Until I see proof to the contrary, though, I'm going to have to assume you still don't have any common sense."

That was as close to truce as his mother was going to get. He could fight about it some more, but fighting with her never got anywhere. He'd inherited her stubbornness, but not as much of it. He shrugged and managed a smile. "Okay. I didn't want to come over to argue with you, anyway. Mostly I just wanted to visit."

She smiled. "Then let's visit."

They chatted for the next hour, staying away from risky topics; Dan told her about his most recent dates with Meg and Janna, and kept her amused with funny stories from the station. When he checked his watch again, he discovered it was time to make a graceful exit and beat a quick retreat before he had to make pleasant chitchat with Arthur. He said, "Ooops! Didn't realize it was so late. Gotta run, Mom—I have an unbelievable amount of work waiting for me."

She stood and walked him to the door, and gave him a quick hug. "Don't forget to call your sister," she said as he headed out the door.

"Why? What's going on?"

"Amy's birthday party, remember? Your niece is going to be how old?"

"Thirty-seven?"

"I said your niece, not your mother, dear."

Dan let his tongue hang out the side of his mouth and panted. "Duuuuh . . . three?"

"Very good. Now don't forget, we'll be expecting you."

Chapter 9

Honorial muttered, "Either there's something wrong with the equipment or we have a problem."

Galas said, "The *equipment* checks out. Our body tracers show over two hundred thousand Hellraised. If you want an *exact* count, I can get it, but it won't hold long. The numbers seem to be increasing."

"They should be decreasing. Scan for total population," Honorial said.

Galas scanned, then sighed. "Just over five million. That's the number our database says we ought to find."

"That's how many there were when the Hellraised got there."

"That's how many there are now, too. What's the fuss?"

"Scan for human population."

Galas kept quiet for a moment. Then he said, "Oh, dear. That's interesting."

"What?"

"We seem to have *misplaced* about two hundred thousand people."

Honorial snapped his badge of rank, his golden quill, into little pieces and flung them to the floor. "God *damn* them!" he snarled.

"*That* would be redundant." Galas smiled, pleased with his little joke.

"Don't you get it? Lucifer's hordes have found a way

to cheat on their numbers. The legitimate population of North Carolina is falling, but somehow the Hellraised have managed to fill in those slots one-for-one without us catching on. They're only supposed to make up one percent of the population. They're way over their allotted numbers."

Galas leaned back in his chair and locked his long fingers behind his head. "Then, *Honorial*, for all intents and *purposes*, the deal ought to be *off*. Right? *They* flagrantly broke their part of the deal. *We* caught them. When we tell Our Munificent Creator, he'll make the misbegotten *fiends* march themselves *straight* back to Hell. And that will be *the end* of the experiment."

Honorial nodded. "Maybe."

"Don't be dramatic. The Holy of Holies *made* his point. You can't *tell* me you think he'll let the experiment continue when he finds out the legions of the damned have been . . . *cheating*."

In fact, Honorial could have told Galas just that. He didn't intend to—for one thing, Galas wouldn't have believed him. For another thing, he simply didn't like Galas very much. But Honorial suspected that, while God might take action to return the excess Hellraised to the nether regions, he didn't think for a moment that the Heavenly One would cancel his joke entirely. He'd been having too much fun with it.

Honorial said, "Give me a printout of this, would you? I'll be talking to God later today—I'd like to be able to show him these numbers." He studied the lesser angel for a moment. "And don't tell anyone else what we've found out here. Please."

"Since *you* ask me, I won't," Galas said, rolling his eyes.

Chapter 10

Dan did remember to call Janna to tell her he would bring Puck by. He had a bit of trouble relocating the devil, though—Puck had said he'd be in the neighborhood of the station if Dan needed him, but Dan's first search didn't turn him up. The sun was setting when Dan spotted Puck and the imp huddled behind the Dumpster in the radio station parking lot. He pulled up near the two Hellraised and watched as they walked past his headlights. The devil was limping.

Dan rolled down the window. "What happened to you?"

Puck shrugged. "Those guys found us again. We camped out under a fire escape in the alley across the street. Bad idea. Fetch slipped away through a sewer grate, but I got caught trying to hop the fence."

"Are you okay?"

"I'll be all right. We heal fast. And it wasn't all one-sided. The fellow with the Louisville slugger sprained his wrist when he broke his bat on my leg."

Dan could understand his fellow humans' revulsion to the filthy, hideous devil. He could even understand their hatred—the Hellraised were, after all, destroying a beautiful state. But he couldn't understand the sort of unquestioning wickedness that permitted human beings to attack creatures they knew were utterly defenseless, no matter how loathsome or vile or evil those creatures might be. Dan only saw violence as a solution in cases of self-defense.

"A girlfriend of mine named Janna offered to help out with the makeover," he said. "She's an actress—did a few pretty decent movies. Sometimes she models. She can teach you how to act in human company—just superficial things, probably, but anything that will make you more acceptable will also lessen the hostility directed toward you. If you aren't so obviously different, maybe people with baseball bats won't keep chasing you around."

"I'm all in favor of that," Puck said, rubbing his leg.

Puck squeaked.

"Good. Then you and Fetch get in."

Puck limped to the car, followed closely by Fetch.

Dan thought while he drove. "Having you living on the street until we find you a place isn't going to work."

"It isn't?"

"No." Dan rolled his window down in spite of the continuing drizzle. "It isn't. For one thing, we can't let a sponsor near you until you smell better."

"I smell bad? I thought the rain gave me a rather fresh scent."

"It does," Dan said. "You smell like fresh shit."

"That's bad?"

Dan glanced over at him to see if the devil was joking. He didn't appear to be. "I think you've been in Hell too long, pal. That's bad."

"Oh."

"So first thing we get to Janna's, you get a bath."

"I thought maybe I could get something to eat."

"That comes afterward. I don't think either of us could stand to eat with you smelling that way. And we'll have to wash your clothes or burn them and let you borrow some of mine. I have a gym bag with some clothes in it in the trunk. I'll take those in and let you wear my gym shorts and a T-shirt when you get out of the bath."

"You don't think your girlfriend will mind me using her bath?"

Dan thought she'd insist, but he didn't say that. "I don't think she'll mind."

A Mercedes idled at the security booth as he pulled up behind it. The guard waved it through, then motioned to the Mustang.

"Your girlfriend lives in a prison?" Puck said.

"It's a gated apartment complex. You have to stop here before going inside." He looked at the guard. "Hi, Wilma."

"Evening, Mr. Cooley. Ms. English told me to expect you. Go right in."

"Thanks."

"Your lady rich?" Puck asked as Dan drove inside.

"Pretty successful."

"And she's dating you?" Puck ran a finger along the dashboard's cracked vinyl and glanced at Dan appraisingly. "You must be hung like a whale."

"Janna appreciates me for my wit and personality."

"Easily satisfied, huh?"

Dan glared at the devil, who retreated.

"Hey, just kidding. Okay?"

Dan found a parking space beside Janna's Corvette. He took out the gym bag and handed it to Puck, then led the way to the elevator, where he noticed that he and the devil were alone. "Where's Fetch?"

"I left it in the car."

"Why?"

"Don't worry. I left the window down a crack."

"I don't think it's a good idea to leave your imp behind."

"Just between you and me, I don't think it's a good

idea to bring it along. Besides, this is the first time it's had someplace safe to sleep in a long time. It spends the nights keeping watch for us."

Dan gave him a distrustful look, but decided against going back to get the imp. Small as it was, he couldn't really see what harm it could do. They got in the elevator, and Dan hit the button for Janna's floor. When it came to a stop and the doors rolled open, they headed down the hallway.

Puck's feet made squishing noises as he walked. Odd, especially once Dan noticed that he wasn't wearing shoes.

"Are we going to eat soon?" Puck asked.

Dan couldn't help grinning as the devil's stomach rumbled. It made a sound like, "Mroooooaaaarrw."

"Soon. Now listen, these are the rules: No foul language, and no lewd gestures or comments. In short, behave yourself."

They stopped in front of the apartment and Puck grinned at him. "So peeing in the fondue is out of the question?"

"You know, there might just be hope for you yet."

The devil looked hurt. "Hey, I'm no hick. I'm sophisticated." He blew his nose in his hand and wiped it on the wall beside Janna's door frame.

Dan winced, then rang the bell. "Charming."

"Anything else?" Puck grinned at him.

"I don't think so," Dan said. "Let's quit while we're not so far behind."

Locks rattled and the door opened.

Janna smiled out at him—the smile was worth a million dollars, easy, and he couldn't figure out why she wasn't in New York or California raking in the dough. She wore sneakers and jeans and one of his oxford shirts with the sleeves rolled up; she had her cornsilk-gold hair pulled back in a ponytail that emphasized her blue eyes. Dan could see the pale red glow of lipstick still staining her lips, but her face was clean-scrubbed. The thing he liked the most about her was that she wasn't always "on," always projecting. Sometimes she seemed a little actressy to him, but most of the time she was just a nice, intelligent woman with a pretty good sense of humor and a fair amount of ambition. He wasn't entirely sure what she saw in him, but he was grateful for whatever it was.

Janna grinned as she noticed the expression on his face. She leaned forward and kissed him gently on the mouth. "Hi," she said. The scent of Georgio Red brushed against him for an instant, reminding him of things more pleasant and wonderful than the devil stench that was inescapable even on the open-air breezeway.

"Hi, yourself."

She turned to the devil then. "So you're Puck." She held out her hand, straightforward, and smiled with what Dan recognized as her professional face.

After an instant's hesitation, the devil held out his own hand. "I'm Puck."

"And I'm Janna." The faintest hint of a pained expression flashed through her eyes, then vanished. "And we have some work to do."

Dan nudged Puck forward and followed him. As they stepped through the door, Janna's dog started yapping.

Puck stared down at him. The dog took no notice of the devil, though. It came straight at Dan, yipping and snarling, and attached itself to his ankle.

"Bits, dammit, *down*!" Janna said.

"Vicious rat you have there," the devil told her.

She picked up the teacup Chihuahua and thumped it on the top of the head. "Yeah," she agreed. "His name is Sir Reginald Bits of Gold—he's a champion, though you would never guess by looking at him. My mother breeds them—she gave him to me for my birthday a couple of years ago."

"Why?" Puck asked.

"I've asked myself the same question more than once." Janna carried the dog into the kitchen, closed the door, and came back out, brushing her hands on her jeans.

"I told Puck he would have to have a bath before supper," Dan said.

"I think a shower would probably work better to start with." Janna eyed the devil. "I don't want rings around the tub that I have to rub off with sandpaper. So why don't you show him into the bathroom and acquaint him with the plumbing, and I'll finish up with supper."

Dan made sure that Puck understood how the plumbing worked and introduced him to soap and shampoo. The devil turned the hot water all the way on and skipped the cold entirely. Dan was going to say something, then decided against it. Puck was probably getting the equivalent of a cold shower as it was.

Once he was sure the devil wasn't going to do something stupid, he laid out the gym clothes and went out to keep Janna company. He had no intention of sticking around to watch Puck undress.

She was waiting in the living room when he came out. "He's showering?"

"He was getting ready to get in when I left."

Janna said, "Everything is in the oven. We have about half an hour before I have to do anything with it. Why don't we go out on the balcony?"

"The weather stinks."

"But the air doesn't."

Dan nodded. Now that she mentioned it, the stench of unwashed devil still clogged the room. He imagined it had to be worse for Janna—she hadn't spent time in a control booth with Puck. Her sense of smell wouldn't be deadened.

He noticed that she left the sliding door open when they stepped outside. "Maybe it won't be so bad when we go back in," he said.

"I didn't want to be rude. I don't know what sort of conditions he's been living in, or how hard things might have been for him. But another minute of that and I would have lost my lunch."

"The whole lettuce leaf?"

Janna grinned. "And the slice of lemon. What are you going to do with him, Dan?"

"I'm going to take him home, let him and his imp sleep on my couch, and hope that regular meals, regular baths, and a little kindness start making a difference in both of them."

"Can't the station find them a place to stay?"

"No. Financially, WKTU is sliding downhill fast. Maybe a sponsor will offer something once this starts taking off. Meanwhile, I'm going to need to put him up. This whole project won't work if he has to live out on the street."

Janna leaned against the wall and watched the rain, which had finally slackened to a drizzle. Dan watched Janna. Pretty, funny, intelligent, ambitious—not too many more things a man could ask for in a woman. He liked holding her—liked the way she smelled and the way she felt. Her unending worries about her appearance seemed typical of other models and actresses he'd known, but she lacked the narcissism that made so many of them unappealing. She was fun to be with.

He prodded at his feelings the way he'd probed the spaces in his mouth when he'd lost teeth as a kid. He felt like he was sliding his tongue into one of those gaps, expecting to find something and finding an emptiness instead. His feelings seemed to consist entirely of his enjoyment of her companionship and his hope that he wouldn't do something to hurt her. And that occasional pang of loss when he looked at her and saw Francie. Maybe he needed to give the relationship more of a chance. Maybe he needed to push for it. He tried to imagine her in goalie pads and a face mask, making a stick save in the driveway, but somehow he couldn't. He wondered if she was standing there thinking about him—if she wondered when he was going to start getting serious.

"I think I can get us paper and television coverage for this makeover," she said.

Oh. Evidently she wasn't thinking about the relationship. He said, "That would be useful."

"Yes." She stood silently for a long time. "Do you think it will work? Do you think your devil in there is actually redeemable?"

He considered that. "I don't know. I really don't. But I have to take the chance that he is. The state is dying, and this is the only thing that I can think of that I can do that might save it."

Chapter 11

God pulled on a tennis shoe, seeming not to listen as Honorial went through the details of Hellish cheating he'd uncovered. "As humans have been leaving the state, the Hellraised Fallen and the devils who were sufficiently high ranking to be able to change their appearances and who were already in the state have been assuming their identities. This has had the effect of fooling our data collection program into thinking the population steady, and allowing Lucifer to send in new Hellraised. The number of Hellraised operating in North Carolina is now far above one percent of the state's total human population."

When the Chief of Data Processing finished his report, God said, "We had to expect that. They're the damned, after all. Expecting them to play by the rules would be expecting the impossible."

"Well, yes . . ." Honorial wasn't hearing the outrage he'd hoped for. "That's what they are . . . but they should have to be held accountable for their actions. Shouldn't they?"

God glanced up at him with a curious expression on his face, one that gave Honorial shivers. "They're condemned to Hell, Honorial. They're damned. If they don't repent, they're damned for eternity. Just what sort of further punishment did you have in mind?

How much more accountable can I make them?"

"So are you going to banish them all back to Hell?"

"That's your recommendation?" God pulled on the other tennis shoe.

Honorial nodded. "Yes, Glorious Almighty."

"I see." God was still giving him that intense look. "Even though we're still getting repenters from among the Hellraised as well as human souls that previously were heading toward damnation, you feel that this infraction is serious enough to warrant an end to the experiment."

"Well . . . yes. Our percentage of North Carolinian human repenters is falling."

"Might that be due to the overall decrease in the human population in the state?"

Honorial winced. He hadn't considered that possibility. "It might."

"Until this experiment started, how many years had it been since we had a repenting fallen angel?"

"I . . . don't believe we've ever had one."

"You're mistaken. We had one. One, and that was six thousand four hundred thirty-two years ago. Earth time. Somewhat before your stint as recording angel began. How many have we had since the experiment started?"

"Twelve."

"Twelve. In eight months. And a couple who are in the middle, trying to work things out. Including, lest you forget, Hell's previous second-in-command. And what about the damnedsouls in all their variety?"

"Repenters?"

God nodded.

"More than a million in the last eight months."

"That's up, isn't it?"

"A little."

"A lot." God raised an eyebrow. "Any changes in the mix?"

"The mix?"

"The percentage of low-ranking to high-ranking damned."

"Oh." Honorial said, "Low-ranking repenters have remained steady. Higher-ranking repenters are trending upward."

"Why?"

Honorial hated that question. "I'm not sure."

"Think it might have anything to do with my experiment?"

Honorial nodded. "But . . . Your Gloriousness . . . they're *cheating*. And if you allow them to get away with it, they'll find other ways to cheat."

God said slowly, "There has never been a time, Honorial, when individuals didn't matter more to me than rules. And I have not, at this late date, had a change of heart." He stood and tucked his T-shirt into his running shorts and brushed a hand across his face. When he did, his beard disappeared. He ran his fingers through his hair and suddenly it was short and neatly trimmed. The glow that always surrounded his face when he was in Heaven vanished. "If that's all, I'm going to go running for a while."

Honorial realized he was about to lose his audience. "If you're going to leave the Hellraised in North Carolina, and if you're going to let them cheat, why don't you at least help out your human children—"

God held up a hand and Honorial stopped. "I don't intervene directly with my children's lives. I don't meddle."

"You could do so much for them, though."

"I could do everything for them," God said softly. "And if I did everything for them, they'd turn into a bunch of whining, sniveling, spoiled monsters; they would have no backbone, no conscience, no morality, no compassion. Souls don't grow in easy times, Honorial. In easy times, they rest. Only when they're challenged with grief and pain and fear and suffering do souls stretch out and reach their potential." He paused, and stared down at his shoes. "Or fail. But my children must be permitted their failures, too."

Honorial watched God walk away. "You already knew what I was going to tell you, didn't you?"

"Yes."

"Why did you wait for me to tell you, then?"

God turned back for just an instant and looked at him. "Sometimes I hope to see signs of growth in my children here, too."

Honorial felt a knot growing inside, and the feeling began to form in him, as he watched God leave, that he had somehow disappointed Him. That God had expected better of him than what He got. He closed his eyes, feeling the unfamiliar heat of shame burning in his cheeks, and was not even sure why he felt it.

Chapter 12

Puck looked better when he came out of the bathroom. He smelled better, too. Dan studied him, wondering why the devil seemed so much more presentable. His wiry hair, fluffed out a little, made his horns look smaller. His teeth didn't seem so sharp. His coppery scales seemed both more attractive and less obvious. A shower and a change of clothing couldn't have done all of that.

Janna was smiling. "Puck, I can't believe it's you."

"I feel . . . better," he said. "This is a very kind thing you're doing for me. It's been a long time since I felt better," he added, sotto voce.

Janna glanced at Dan, her eyebrows raised. Dan said, "Well, you'll feel even better after a meal."

The three of them sat at the table. Janna showed Puck the knife, forks and spoons, and took a moment to show him how he needed to hold each.

Then she brought out the food. Puck's brightened demeanor vanished in an instant. "What's all this?"

"Stuffed tomatoes, eggplant parmesan, three-bean salad, and carrot sticks," Janna said. "I thought I'd keep it simple."

The devil stared at the food in dismay. "Don't you have anything that bleeds when you cut it?"

"Meat?"

"Well, turnips don't bleed."

"Ugh! No!" Janna wrinkled her nose. "Didn't Dan tell you I'm a vegetarian?"

The devil gave Dan a cold look. "He forgot to mention that."

"Well, I am. And if I cook, I cook vegetarian for everybody."

"If you'd cooked a vegetarian, I wouldn't be complaining," Puck said.

Dan covered his mouth with a hand. "No, Puck. Funny joke, but not here."

Puck leaned over and whispered, "Who was joking?"

This isn't going to work, Dan thought. He motioned for Puck to sit down, then joined him. He leaned over and whispered in Puck's ear, "This is the food you get. You don't have to like it. Just eat it."

"Did I forget to mention to you that I'm a pure carnivore?" Puck whispered back. "I eat this vegetable slop and it's going to go straight through me and come out the other end looking exactly the same as it does now."

Dan stared at him. The devil shrugged.

"What about cheeses?"

"I can tolerate those, but I *much* prefer raw meat. The fresher the better."

Dan closed his eyes. It had to figure, didn't it? He told Puck, "She doesn't have any meat. Eat the cheese off of the eggplant parmesan and don't worry about the rest. We'll get something you'll like better on the way home."

Janna instructed the devil on the proper use of napkins (It's what you just used your sleeve for) and silverware (Don't stab, Puck; I assure you that the cheese is quite dead).

Dan and Janna started a conversation—how their workdays went, what sort of things they anticipated for the evening. Puck tried, gamely, to join in. The results were awful.

"I used to have a game I liked to play," he said, when Janna said she really would love to play a set of tennis with Dan.

"Really?" She gave him a smile, the one with the raised eyebrows that Dan always saw as her polite "I'm listening" smile. Puck had quit even pretending to eat. He'd been sitting quietly staring at his plate.

"Yeah," he said. "In Hell, I used to be on chute duty with a couple of other guys and we always had this game. New damnedsouls come in with their Evilness Index stamped on their heads. You know: four fifty-three or seven twenty . . . like that. Some of them come in ready to be devils or demons—you know, pretty high on the food chain—while some are never going to be anything but imps or leccubi or gargoyles. So the other demons and I—this was before I made devil—we'd agree on a number each day, something between two hundred and a thousand; those are the numbers on the Evilness Index that will end you up in Hell—and then we'd go through the new souls and the one that was closest to the number we picked, we'd misfile. This one guy, he'd come in as a first-level devil—his index was about eight hundred." Puck started laughing. "It was the funniest damned thing. He would have been our boss, but we made him into a gargoyle." He was sputtering and thumping his hands on the table by that time. "And gargoyles are gargoyles forever! They can't advance!" Puck suddenly realized neither Dan nor Janna was laughing, and his own laughter died. "See," he said, "it was a practical joke. It was funny. He was all set to be this powerful guy in Hell, and now he's stuck forever being a gargoyle . . ."

Dan kept staring at him, unable to think of anything to say.

"What?" Puck's voice rose defensively. "Are you trying to tell me you don't think that was funny?"

Dan and Janna exchanged glances, and Janna finally answered. "I think you'd probably be better off, Puck, if you didn't tell any more work-related stories until you get a job other people can relate to."

"Oh." He looked down at his plate again. "I see. Your stupid story about an actor saying his lines wrong fifty times in a row was funny, and his stupid story about the caller who couldn't get the joke right and kept forgetting the ending was funny, but my story, which *really happened*, wasn't funny."

Dan shook his head. "I think you might want to avoid humor until you have a better feel for it."

Puck looked at him coldly. "Yeah. I'll keep that in mind." He gulped the contents of his glass, then looked at Janna. "You mind if I get myself something else to drink?"

"Not at all." Janna pointed to the closed kitchen door. "Right in there. Help yourself to whatever you want."

Dan could tell Janna felt guilty about not being able to laugh at Puck's story. When Puck left the room, she turned to him and sighed. "I think he wants to fit in, Dan, but if he tells stories like that at dinner, no one is going to want to have anything to do with him. He'll never be accepted."

"I know."

A loud crash—followed by a high-pitched yip—erupted from the kitchen.

Janna shot to her feet so fast her chair fell backwards. She ran into the kitchen with Dan half a step behind her.

He froze just inside the door. "Oh, no."

Puck stood in front of the open refrigerator, his neck bulging. One hind leg and a short, ratlike tail hung out of his mouth. As Dan watched in horror, the devil swallowed convulsively and the Chihuahua's hindquarters slipped down his throat like a rat down a snake's gullet.

"He bit me, I bit him," the devil said.

Chapter 13

Meg got home late. She'd spent much of her day at the Raleigh office of the ACLU, going over case law with an old colleague.

Her uncle Ed greeted her at the door. "Thanks so much for calling. Supper's burned."

"I'm sorry I didn't call. I simply could not get to a phone." Meg shoved her hair back from her face and kicked her shoes into the hall closet. "Who cooked?"

"What difference does that make?"

"I want to know whether to weep or rejoice that I was late."

"Greg cooked."

"So I have to weep." She sighed. "I'll do it later, okay? Right now I'm too tired to cry."

"Dare I hope that you're working for a paying customer?" He led them into the kitchen and pulled out a seat for her before getting one for himself.

She dropped into it and rested her elbows on the table. Only when she completely settled in could she feel the ache in her back and the back of her neck, or appreciate how completely beat she was. "Nope. Something speculative."

"Oh. Wonderful. And how shall *speculative* pay the rent?"

Meg eyed him warily. He wore a half-smile on his face

but it wasn't the sort of half-smile she'd come to associate with encouragement. It was more along the lines of "Meg's lost her mind again; what is she thinking this time?" She said, "I wanted to talk to you about that."

"I'm sure."

"This . . . case . . . has the potential to turn the situation in North Carolina around."

"I see. You're petitioning God for a miracle. And for that I'm expected to forgo another month of rent on your room."

"Well, it would help a lot." Meg sighed. "I know this is awkward. But listen. I think I have the solution to all of North Carolina's problems with the Hellraised." She shook her head and waved a hand in negation. "Let me try that again. I think I may have a partial solution that could greatly lessen North Carolina's problems with the Hellraised. I don't want to allow myself to fall into hyperbole."

"Never that," her uncle said, and rolled his eyes. "So what is this tremendous idea?"

"I want to work with my old colleagues in the ACLU to file an antidiscrimination suit on behalf of North Carolina's Hellraised."

Ed's eyes widened. "You want to do *what*?" That response, at least, was pure disbelief, completely without the affectation of ennui that Ed put into almost everything else.

"I want the ACLU to file an antidiscrimination suit on behalf of North Carolina's Hellraised," Meg repeated.

"Dear God. Megan, half the people in this state are already convinced lawyers are in league with Satan. You want to prove their case?"

"Ed, hear me out. There's a method to my madness."

He nodded. "My meticulous lunatic. I'll wager your friends always refer to you as the quiet one."

"Depended on what kind of friends they are. Come on. Give me a chance to explain."

"Dar-r-r-rling . . . as if I'd let you leave this room without an explanation."

She perched on the edge of her seat and leaned forward. "Answer me this. What happens when two hostile and disparate cultures are forced to coexist due to mutual self-interest?"

"Bosnia. The Democratic party."

She ignored the jibe. "Two things can happen. Either the two integrate, forming a new culture, or they clash, and one culture is destroyed."

Ed rested his chin in his hand. Withholding commitment, she thought. "Humans and the Hellraised. I see where you think you're going, but in this case your point doesn't apply. The Hellraised are incapable of harming human beings. And, from what I understand, there isn't a great deal we can do to them either."

"Exactly! So what is the result?"

He thought for a moment. "Continuous conflict."

"With no peace for anyone. And remember, while the Hellraised can't directly harm us, they can create situations where we might harm one another, by using our own stupidity and prejudices against us."

"No one denies that the Hellraised can be dangerous."

"And will continue to be so. Unless an alternative exists."

Meg watched his brow furrow. Good, that means he's intrigued. "What kind of alternative?" he said.

"You remember Glenda, the ACLU paralegal I got along with so well? She and I did a search of the Internet and found and downloaded the contract that God—or Heaven—made with the Hellraised. It's short, to the point, and as far as I can tell, rife with loopholes."

"You have a copy."

"You bet." She dug the folded paper from her pants pocket and unfolded the single-spaced pages. She studied them again briefly, still unable to believe what she'd found. The complete printout read:

From: honorial@data_proc.chrstn.hvn.aftrlif.net (Honorial, Chief of Data Processing, HeavenNet)
Received: from hellex.hellwire.info.net by x1.hellwire.info.net for <lucifer.the.fallen@chrstn.hell.aftrlif.net>; Fri, 8, Oct 15:14:10 -0400)
Received from HEAVEN.aftrlif.net by x1.hellwire.info.net; Fri, 8, Oct 14:17:41 -0500
Return path: honorial@data.proc.chrstn.hvn.aftrlif.net
To: lucifer.the.fallen@chrstn.hell.aftrlif.net
Subject: Operation Tarheel
Message-ID: <9605181666.ZZ131313HEAVEN.aftrlif.net>

- -

Command from On High

By order of the God of Heaven and Earth, Creator of All Things, Eternal Parent of the Infinities, Bringer of Joy and Hope, Master of all the Realms—

O fallen angel who is anathema to me, you whose name shall not pass my lips until you have humbled yourself before me—

By my order and on my express command and through the intercession of my daughter, Dayne Teresa Kuttner, you shall send forth out of Hell, under my parole, exactly fifty-eight thousand eight hundred fifty-one fallen angels, devils, demons, and assorted members of the lower orders of Hell's crawling vermin into the state of North Carolina — this number being exactly one one-hundredth of the human population in that state at the instant of my reckoning.

Unchained denizens of Hell must obey the following rules:

- They will neither inflict, nor pay to have inflicted, any physical harm on any human.
- They will not parent a child with a

human, either with or without the human's consent.

- They will not steal by supernatural means.
- They will not cause any disease or plague, nor will they act as the agents through which any disease or plague is transmitted.
- They will not impersonate a minister, God, or angel of God, or any divine messenger of God.
- They will not cause any virgin births.
- They will not leave the State of North Carolina.

The Unchained denizens of Hell may:

- Lie, tempt, deceive, mislead, and otherwise carry out the usual agenda of Hell.
- Impersonate human beings if that is within their nature and capacity.
- Own property, become citizens, hold offices, own and operate legal businesses, marry humans – if the humans are apprised of their true nature beforehand and no intimidation is used – and in all other legal ways approved by the State of North Carolina attempt to achieve a normal life on Earth.
- Enter into binding contracts with human beings – with one of the two following stipulations:

  1) The human must be fully apprised of the nature of the contract and the nature of all parties involved in the contract; or,

  2) The human must sign the contract with his own blood. (Percentage of blood to inert materials not specified; blood must be less than twenty-four hours old in Earth-sequential time

```
      only, as per previous agreements
      between Heaven and Hell; human must
      know that blood has been drawn; no
      blood from blood donorship or other
      merciful blood collection agencies,
      or from accidents and injuries may
      be used.)
  -  Repent.
Unchained denizens of Hell must:
  -  Eat and drink mortal food, or their
     Earthly bodies will wither and fail,
     and they will have to pay Heaven for
     new ones. Heaven will charge a cost-
     per-body fee plus punitive wastage tax
     for any Earthly bodies above and beyond
     the one that will be issued free from
     Heaven per Hell-soul at the time of
     exit from Hell - this will be collected
     by the usual revenue methods. These
     Heaven-issued Earth-bodies will be
     indistinguishable from the individual
     Hellspawn's normal form and will have
     all the Hellspawn's usual abilities
     excluding those which would run counter
     to the above decrees.
  -  Obtain their sustenance in the normal
     mortal way - that is, by growing food
     or paying for it with cash or barter.
```

Meg shook her head and handed the document over to her uncle.

Ed read over it, his expression more bemused by the second. "I wonder if it's legitimate."

"As far as anyone could tell, it was. The appended text at the top of the file, which I didn't print, said something about a hacker who received a post not too long after the Unchaining that had been routed through hellwire.info.net, who started trying to e-mail the addresses until he finally got an answer. According to the post, Heaven didn't get back to him, though his message didn't bounce, so he assumed it was received. Hell, however, sent proselytizers to his door and put him on all its mailing lists and kept finding him no matter how often he changed his e-mail address. He finally, according to the story, had to drop off the Internet entirely and move out of state."

"I've ended up on mailing lists like that," Ed said.

"Someone told the Jehovah's Witnesses once that I wanted personal visitation; I've always suspected it was the husband of a client of mine whose divorce I handled. That was almost as bad. Anyway, the stipulations that I find most interesting are those that suggest the Hellraised have permission to settle down and live normal lives here—and the hardcopy proof that they're allowed to repent."

"Why?"

"Because if they're given a chance to live normal lives, maybe they'll repent. If they repent, they aren't a problem anymore. I want to tie in this lawsuit with the devil who is participating in the Great Devil Makeover at WKTU."

"I thought that was a publicity stunt."

Meg shrugged. "It might have been, though Dan sounded sincere when he talked it up on his show. I still have to discuss this with Dan, and with the devil, whose name is Puck. I have to assume that Puck is a likely candidate for repentance—he's been given a second chance here on Earth and if I can take the calls Dan fielded over the air as any indication, he has a lot of people who are rooting for him."

"That's hard to imagine."

"People want to be able to hope that things will get better. If he defects, they can work toward gaining other defectors." Meg leaned forward in her chair, excited all over again in spite of her weariness. "To encourage this, we have to sweeten the pot as much as possible. First, he must be able to hold a job. A legal one. He needs to get a green card or a social security number, pay taxes, contribute to the welfare of the state. He needs to have a place to live that he can pay for himself. An antidiscrimination suit and some good publicity will help a great deal."

Ed sat in the chair across from her, his eyes closed.

"What do you think?"

He shook his head. "Give me some time, Meg."

"How about the rent?"

He sighed. "I'll let it go another month. This at least pretends to be a worthy cause, though I don't imagine you'll accomplish anything."

"Thanks."

Greg came into the kitchen, kissed Meg on the top of the head, and kissed Ed in passing. "Couldn't you even take it out for her?"

"I didn't want to feed her madness." When Greg gave him raised eyebrows, Ed said, "She's lost her mind. I was just listening to the tale."

Greg grinned at Meg. "You want to hear about lost minds, you should have Eddie tell you about his day."

Meg raised an eyebrow. "Bad?"

"Worse than usual. One of my bank tellers is almost due. The vixen waited until today to tell me she'll be taking twelve weeks of family leave after the birth. My chief loan officer is still laid up with a broken leg, so the bank is shorthanded for the rest of the month."

She winced. Ed's bank was busy with a full complement of staff—one of the few businesses in Raleigh that hadn't suffered a severe drought after the advent of the Hellraised. "Sorry. I know how hard that makes things."

Greg placed a plate in front of her, then took a chair

next to Ed and rested his head on Ed's shoulder. "We've been up to our asses in alligators today."

Meg started eating. The food melted in her mouth. She murmured, "God, Greg, when are you going to open your own restaurant?"

He laughed. "Probably when Hell goes back where it belongs. Eddie's not exactly being loose with his venture capital right now."

Meg laughed. "He's a Republican, Greg. He was born being tight with his money."

"That's why I still have some."

Meg smiled at her uncle. "I know." A thought occurred to her. "Um . . . with you being shorthanded at the bank right now, what do you think the chances are that you might be able to give Dan's devil a job?"

"The proverbial snowflake in Hell would do better."

"Yeah. I thought I'd ask anyway. Do you know anyone who might give him a job?"

"Well, the IRS is always looking for a few good men."

"Not funny."

"I thought it was."

"He'll need to do something that will improve his reputation, not make it worse." Meg sighed. "You know more about the business community than anyone I know. Assuming they sought employment, what are the chances the Hellraised could find jobs?"

"Microscopic at best." Ed rubbed his chin. "They'll have to manage in the traditional 'unwelcome immigrant' fashion."

"Which is?"

"Go into business for themselves."

"Where would they get the money?"

Ed leaned back in his chair and closed his eyes for a moment. Then he looked over at her and smiled. "Now I can give you good news. I know people who would offer their firstborn as collateral if there is profit to be made. And if the right opportunity came along."

"We'll be trying to avoid deals of that nature, but if you can keep those people in mind, and if, after I've talked with Dan and Puck, I can come up with a suitable project, would you help me put it together?"

"For the good of the state—and my own business, of course—I'll certainly consider it."

Chapter 14

"I can't blame you," Dan said as he drove them to his apartment. "I've wanted to kill that little rat ever since I met it. I'm tempted to pay you for having done me a favor."

The devil sat in the car, staring out the window. "It was reflex. Plus I was hungry—and it smelled delicious."

"I really do understand. But this is going to make things difficult for me with Janna." He sighed. "Still, knowing that little shit won't piss in my shoe or bite my ankle again, I'm inclined to do something really nice for her to see if I can't make up."

"Like what?"

"I don't know. Buy her some roses? Find her a kitten? Yeah, that's a decent idea. I *like* cats."

"So do I."

Dan glanced at Puck. "The same way you like dogs?"

Puck sighed. "Well . . . yes."

"Great. If I get her a kitten, don't eat it. Okay?"

"Okay."

Chapter 15

Lucifer's new lieutenant, Garafanal, stood at his lord's left hand in the throne room, after the last of the newly damned were led out and sent to their stations. Lucifer sensed that some new envy ate at Garafanal, but he couldn't quite guess what.

He turned to the fallen angel, who stood stiffly, staring straight ahead, and said, "All day there has been something you've wanted to say to me. All day. It's impinged on your performance. Yet you haven't said anything to me."

Garafanal nodded. "I doubted that you would care to hear my concerns."

"You're probably right. Nevertheless, tell them to me."

"I wonder at Scumslag's ability to run the North Carolina mission."

"Do you?" Lucifer tapped on the armrest of his red-lacquered seat with long, pointed talons. "And why is that?"

"He's only a devil, Your Loathsomeness."

"I noticed."

"I mean, even if he is a Devil First Class, how could he possibly be as competent as one of the Fallen?"

"Bucking for a trip upstairs?" Lucifer asked.

"Me? To Earth? No, O Mighty Foulness. I never want to leave your presence. I'm just concerned that the mission be successful."

Lucifer laughed. "You don't know anything about Scumslag, do you?"

"Not really."

Lucifer leaned back. "We got him after he died of old age. He was a businessman in a small town—at one time had a wife and three kids. He murdered his wife after her obstetrician told her she couldn't have any more children, then systematically began abusing and molesting the kids. When his oldest, a boy, turned eleven, he threw him down the stairs and killed him because he threatened to tell. The other two shut up. Neither of them ever came forward. The middle child, a girl, ran away when she was thirteen, became a prostitute in Richmond, Virginia, and died of a drug overdose at fifteen. The youngest boy also ran away, but he found help. I'd hoped he would turn out like his father, but he's been such a disappointment."

Garafanal shrugged. "I could pick out fifteen thousand damnedsouls with stories just like his."

"Could you?" Lucifer smiled. "With his youngest son gone, this man started collecting young boys, runaways mostly, but the occasional child from the town. He molested, tortured and murdered the boys and buried them in the backyard. The family who bought the house and lives there now has no idea. They're considering putting in a garden next spring, though—I'm looking forward to their first crop." Lucifer chuckled.

"Fine. He was evil—"

"Evilness Index of nine hundred sixty. One of the highest we've ever received."

Garafanal stubbornly kept going. "—But surely one of the Fallen would be better in the administrative role in which you've placed him."

"He has an MBA. He built up his own business from nothing. And even more importantly, he spent his entire life mixing with the people of the small town where he lived his whole life. He was a Jaycee and later a Shriner; he raised money for the Children's Christmas Fund; he belonged to the country club and lived in a good neighborhood and drove a nice car. No one ever suspected him of anything. He knows the rules of the game they play up there better than anyone." Lucifer rested a hand on Garafanal's shoulder and smiled down at him. "The Fallen lack that sort of practical Earthside experience. You're theoreticians, and I've had evidence that your theories don't always hold up terribly well in practice."

"Agonostis was weak."

"Agonostis held the job you now hold for millennia. He wasn't weak. He simply wasn't right for the job. I've learned," Lucifer said, letting go of Garafanal's shoulder, and noticing absently the charred handprint he left behind, "that I must set a thief to catch a thief."

Chapter 16

WEDNESDAY, JUNE 8TH

Dan rolled over and opened one eye only enough to catch the green glow of the clock radio.

Seven A.M.? *Seven* A.M.?!

In the instant when he was certain that his alarm had failed to go off and that he was late for work—really, really late—his entire body tensed, his heart raced and his mouth went drier than North Carolina pavement on a hot day in August. Then he relaxed. Day off, he thought. Day off. Day off. He willed his heart to slow down, reminding himself that he wasn't late. Day off. He had a glorious day alone, with nothing to do but sleep, or watch television, or kick around town looking for a movie that was worth seeing.

He let go of his tension. He breathed in and out slowly, and like a cat, stretched his entire body and yawned, feeling every muscle pull deliciously. When he finished, he wrapped his arms around his pillow and curled on one side. The waterbed shifted around him, conforming, seeming to blend with him until his awareness of it as a thing apart from himself disappeared, the bed temperature, neither too cool nor too warm, lulled him. He drifted in a soothing, linen-scented, floating half-dream lit by the soft warm fall of dappled sunlight through patterned curtains. . . .

"YOU'RE GOING TO BE LATE!"

The bellow, next to his ear, shocked him out of his fetal curl. He tried to bound upright but the waterbed confounded him, sinking under him where he most needed resistance, rising up where he most needed clearance. The sheets came to life, rolling around him and tangling his flailing legs, until, flopping like a fish, he heaved himself over the side of the bed, and trailing sheets and comforter and pillows, crashed to the floor.

A devil stood over him. Oh. Right. *Puck* stood over him, grinning slightly, shaking his head, gleaming like an oversized, butt-ugly penny. "You okay?"

Dan rubbed his head. "Other than the concussion, you mean? Yeah, I'm swell." He looked up at the devil. "What are you doing in my room?"

"It's after seven; you're going to be late for work." Puck motioned toward the shower with his thumb.

"Puck, before the temptation to strangle you overcomes me, I should tell you that today is my day off."

"Yeah? Yesterday your boss' secretary told me that I had to be kind of presentable because today you were going to take me to meet sponsors for a couple of . . . on-site promotions?"

Shit, Dan thought. He's right. I was supposed to call in and find out which sponsors were willing to meet with him.

"You're right. I forgot. Give me a minute to get showered and changed. You can borrow some of my clothes . . . you sure can't go in the shorts and T-shirt."

"Why not?"

"Because it shows too much of you, Puck. Way too much. The less anyone can see of you, the better. If we could hide your face under a paper bag, we'd be in there." He sighed and untangled himself from the sheets.

"Dammit. And I was ready to sleep, too." He climbed to his feet. "Puck?"

"What?"

Dan pointed at his bedroom door, which stood ajar. "Don't come in here without knocking. Okay?"

"That was wrong?"

Dan nodded emphatically. "Way wrong. Always knock on a closed door before you enter it."

The devil nodded. "Sorry. I didn't realize that was wrong. We don't have doors in Hell. Well," he shrugged. "We do, but they aren't doors anyone would want to be behind. And the people who go through them don't come back out. Doors are still a bit of an awkward concept for me."

"S'alright."

Dan shaved and took a quick shower. He spent more time than usual picking out his clothes. The local businessmen weren't impressed by his usual look—loud Hawaiian shirts and khakis. No pleasing some people. But he had a couple of silk shirts—one of those would work. Something light-colored, he thought; after all, the rain had stopped, the sun was back, and by noon it was going to be hotter than . . .

Well. No, it wouldn't. But it would be pretty hot.

He found one in a dusty green. He dug though his jeans until he found a cream-colored pair of chinos. He thought about adding a vest, but decided against it. In fact, he rolled up the sleeves and decided to skip the tie. He was a DJ, after all. People cut him *some* slack. And besides, the night before, Channel Five had predicted the temperature would hit a high of one hundred and one, with eighty percent humidity.

He shoved his wallet into his hip pocket, then went to tell Puck it was his turn in the shower.

"Wha—?"

Dishes, empty and full, covered the dining room table. Puck waved at him. "Hey, come on! We made breakfast for you!"

Oh no, he thought. The kitchen . . .

Puck followed Dan's look. "I wouldn't go in there just yet. But don't worry; the imp will have it clean in no time!"

Dan studied the meal Puck had prepared. Sausage, swimming in grease. Bacon, done to a carbon black.

"What's that?" he asked Puck.

"Huh? Oh, those are eggs."

Dan shook his head. "I've never seen blue eggs before."

"Oh, that was the imp. It got a little crazy with the food coloring." Puck held up a bowl. "Want some grits? They were blue too at first. Then I dumped two sticks of butter in." The devil looked at the bowl. "What color would you call that, exactly?"

"Baby-shit green. Look, Puck, I appreciate the effort, but—ah—I'm not much of a breakfast person."

Puck, crestfallen, studied the food spread across the table. "Oh." He ran a talon across the tablecloth they'd put out (Tablecloth? I don't own a tablecloth.)—across the *bedsheet* they'd put out, and sighed. "You don't mind if *we* eat it, do you?"

Dan spread his arms. "Please. I'd hate to see it all go to waste." Especially since that looks like most of what I had in the fridge. Dan stepped past the table into the kitchen.

"Christ!"

Puck materialized at his shoulder. "Where?!"

Technicolored glop smeared down the walls and across the floor and hung in pendulous globs from the ceiling—one reached the critical breakpoint as Dan glanced at it and dropped to the floor with a *splorch*. Bright orange globlets spattered across the floor and Dan jumped back to avoid being hit. Broken glasses and broken dishes and pans full of burned food filled the sink and overflowed onto the counter. And someone had unrolled an entire roll of toilet paper in great loops across the table, between the table legs and across the spindle arms of the lamp. "It looks like chimpanzees went to war in here. Or like some of my old fraternity buddies dropped by for a drink," he added.

"Well . . ." Puck stared at his feet. "Fetch started it."

"Fetch . . . started . . . it." Dan remembered that tone of voice from his childhood. "*Fetch*, huh? You're supposed to be the responsible one," he said, and immediately wished he hadn't. The line—patently his mother's—sounded wrong coming out of his mouth, and made him feel suddenly old.

"Fetch will fix everything. Might as well start now." Puck walked back into the dining room and picked up the imp by the scruff of its neck. He whispered into its ear, then dropped it to the floor.

The imp squeaked, then dashed by Dan through the doorway.

"It'll be fine, you'll see," Puck said. A loud crash came from the kitchen. "It's really good at putting plates back together too. Come on, sit down and have some coffee."

I don't think they're going to be able to stay with me after all, Dan thought. Maybe the street *would* work until someone else found them a place.

"You know what the problem is with you humans?" Puck poured coffee into Dan's Renaissance Fair mug. "You don't know how easy you've got it. If you had to spend one day in Hell, you'd have a different attitude, let me tell you. Hey, is black okay? We're out of creamer and milk. Oh, and sugar. And bacon, sausage, eggs, flour, orange juice, salt, pepper . . ."

Oh my aching bank account, Dan thought. He took the mug and sipped. "Oh!"

"What's wrong now?"

"Wrong? Nothing." Dan took another swallow. "This is the best coffee I've ever had."

"Yeah, if there's one thing a devil knows about, it's how to apply heat."

"I'll bet." He didn't do anything to encourage that line of conversation, and this time Puck opened his mouth, then closed it again without adding any further insights into his work. When he finished the coffee, he rose and put the cup down on the table.

"Get your shower and put on the clothes I laid out for you. I'll call Darlene and find out who we need to meet today. And hurry, okay? We may need to get on the road right away."

By the time the devil had showered and dressed—dusty pink seersucker jacket, navy shirt, navy tie, and navy slacks—Dan had his day's itinerary. Amazingly, it was a long one. Darlene said everyone at the station had been stunned by the response among advertisers.

He hung up and turned to Puck. "They're ready to give you a chance, man. Let's go."

The devil nodded and shuffled toward the door. Dan noticed his unshod clawed feet—definitely not in keeping with the rest of his look—and sighed. "Shoe store first." He'd keep the receipt and pay for the shoes out of his own pocket.

Halfway down the stairs he remembered the imp. "Wait. We've got to go back."

"Why?"

"Fetch is in the apartment."

"I know. It's still cleaning." Puck grinned, and this time Dan was certain his fangs really were a little smaller. "Don't worry. I told it to scrub the place down, then crawl into the tub until we got back. It won't hurt anything, I swear. Anyway, you don't want it around your sponsors. If it gets excited, no leg is safe. Understand what I'm saying?"

"Oh. Yuck." Terrific, Dan thought. Either he trusted the imp alone in his apartment for the day or he risked ruining the entire Makeover project because it had a penchant for the shin shimmy. His mom always said if no choice was good, to take the lesser of two evils.

Or leave the lesser of two devils.

Or something like that.

"We'll leave it."

"Good. Don't worry! You won't recognize the place when we get back."

Probably not, Dan thought. Probably not.

Chapter 17

"How do you do Mr.—would Puck be your first or last name?"

"Only."

"Mr. Puck. I'm Samuel Offing, owner of Reginald Court Menswear." He held out a hand and the devil, somewhat hesitantly, shook it. "We have the finest men's garments in Raleigh. Historically we have relied on word-of-mouth for our advertising, but recent changes in statewide demographics have required us to be a bit more flexible in our approach."

"He just said all the rich people moved out of state," Puck said to Dan in a stage whisper that Dan was certain Offing couldn't have missed.

Offing's laugh sounded false in Dan's ears. "Precisely."

Dan said, "I understood what he was saying without the translation."

"Sorry."

Offing said, "Please don't worry about it. I understand that Mr. Puck is still . . . ah . . . rough around the edges. But I also understand *your* campaign, Mr. Cooley. I think you have a wonderful idea, and I'd like to help. However, I will expect a significant return on my investment."

Dan nodded and got out one of the station's advertising contracts. "What were you thinking of?"

"First let me tell you what I can do for you. In addition to paying your regular advertising rate for spots, I'll supply a complete wardrobe for Mr. Puck here. Suits, sports clothing, undergarments, appropriate footwear, neckties, hats if he needs them . . . all tailored to emphasize his good points." Offing paused a minute to study Puck. Dan figured he was trying to come up with a good point or two to use as examples. He frowned, shrugged and said, "Or at least deemphasize the worst of his bad points."

"When can you have it for him?"

"I assume you have a full schedule today. If he comes in tomorrow morning, though, early, we'll fit him. I can have some of the wardrobe tomorrow—sportswear won't take much work on our part. The suits I can have in the next several days."

Dan nodded. "That's quite generous. A regular advertising campaign wouldn't cost you as much as a wardrobe of these clothes."

"No. It wouldn't. But I don't want a regular advertising campaign. In exchange for my investment, I want exclusivity. No other clothier, no other clothing advertised in relation to Mr. Puck."

Dan figured out amounts involved, and said, "We'll need a guaranteed number of thirty-second spots per week for the length of the Great Devil Makeover campaign to guarantee exclusivity."

"I'll have my assistant work out the contract details with you. I'll sign your contract after I've had a chance to speak with Mr. Puck."

Dan's eyebrows went up. "Why—"

Offing cut him off. "You say you have a devil who's willing to try to change his ways. Before I risk any of my money, which is increasingly hard to come by, *I* want to feel that there's some chance of his success."

"I'll talk to him," Puck said.

"Fine." Dan shrugged, not really certain that he should turn the devil loose with Offing, but not sure what else he could do. So he went off with the assistant and got the man to agree to an exorbitant amount of advertising.

Offing and Puck, meanwhile, went into the back room.

When they came out, nearly forty-five minutes later, Offing wore a smile Dan could have spotted from across town. He got ready to discuss the contract, but Offing just signed it and said, "Have him in here tomorrow."

Dan glanced at Puck, wondering what the devil had said to so completely reassure the man, then gave him a hard second look. Puck's scales were smaller and finer, and his features seemed a little bit more sculptured . . . a little less like afterthoughts. And he couldn't be sure, but he thought perhaps the claws had become slightly less sharp.

Contract in hand and fitting appointment made, he walked Puck out to the car in silence. Only once they were on the road did he ask.

"What happened in there?"

Puck leaned back in the seat and stared at the road ahead. "His only son died in a car accident last year. Ugly circumstances. He wanted to know if he'd . . . ah . . ."

"Gone to Hell?"

"Yes."

"How could you help him? I thought you said you didn't work in Personnel," Dan said.

"That's right."

"Then how could you know his son isn't in Hell?"

"He had a computer. I'm out of the loop, but I still know the ropes, if you know what I mean."

"Computer?"

"Yes. If you know what you're doing, you can extract data from the HellWire Info Net."

"And what did you find out?"

"That his son wasn't a bad kid. He didn't sign on with us."

"You look different."

"I feel different. I helped him, you know. And I didn't do it to make him buy your station advertising or because I was going to get a bunch of clothes out of him. I did it because . . . because . . ." Puck fell silent.

"Why?"

"I don't know why."

"That's okay. Sooner or later, you'll figure it out."

Chapter 18

Meg slipped off her shoe and thumped a cockroach as it scuttled behind her desk. Then she slipped the flat back on and went through the morning's mail. Bill. Bill. Late check from a client. Letter from a client explaining why check was not enclosed. Bill. Junk.

The phone rang.

"Lerner Family Consulting, may I help you?"

"Meg, it's Ed."

"Hi, Uncle Ed. What's up?"

"I have some news for you."

"Good or bad?"

"Good."

"Then I'll keep you. What's your news?"

"I have your investment group."

"Really? That's outstanding! May I ask whom?"

"Some of my clients at the bank are willing to put together the money to fund a consortium, if you and your devil can come up with the right project."

"How much are they willing to go?"

"We're currently liquid for eight million dollars, and—again for the right project—we can go higher. Here's the stipulation. We're not looking for a long-term investment, but something with a quick turnover. Do you have any idea when you can have a proposal for us?"

Meg remembered the law office where she'd worked while she was getting her degree, and the lawyer who got a call asking if he had any knowledge of publishing law. He'd said yes and set up an appointment for the next day. Meg waited until he was off the phone, then said, "You don't know anything about publishing law."

He said, "I will by tomorrow morning. Expediency rules, Meg. Always take the client. Spend the night studying case law if you must, but *always* take the client."

She didn't agree with him at the time, but now she found herself thinking, Expediency rules. "I'll have it as soon as you're ready to see it. I'm booked today and I have court tomorrow, but if I can set up a meeting with everyone the day after that, I'll put the proposal on the table for you."

"That will be fine. Oh, by the way, I ran into Frances Lederman on the golf course this morning. She wanted to know if there was any chance you'd changed your mind?"

"About the partnership offer? No, I haven't. Corporate stuff just isn't my area of interest. There aren't enough family lawyers with fees real people can afford, so I'm going to stick with my private practice. If I find myself prowling the pet food aisle at the grocery store, I might reconsider. Till then, I'm going to tough it out."

She said her good-byes, then checked her calendar. Bainbridge for a divorce consultation at ten-thirty. Lackland to discuss getting an increase in child support at noon. Simkins at three to work out the last details of a separation agreement. And dinner with Dan and the devil at seven.

Plenty of time in between to work on the legal brief for the class-action antidiscrimination suit. And to figure out some sort of business the Hellraised could do that would be an attractive short-term investment for her uncle's group.

Chapter 19

Dan led the devil into Irregardless on West Morgan Street a few minutes before seven.

"I'd say that went well," Puck said.

"I'd say the whole day went extraordinarily well." When they were seated at a comfortable booth at the back, Dan studied his menu. "Try the Bean Burger," he told the devil. "It's fabulous." He ordered a margarita while he waited for Meg; the devil drank scotch, neat.

Dan put his menu aside. He didn't want to order food until Meg got there. "It was so strange that almost all of them wanted to talk with you first, though."

"Not really. Almost everyone knows someone he cares about who didn't live an exemplary life. Almost everyone would like to know that friend or family member wasn't damned."

Puck had changed remarkably during the day. His manner of speech was gentler. His facial expressions lacked the air of Hellish viciousness they'd had when Dan first found him. And physically he'd become different, too. His copper scales, initially so large and coarse and sharp-edged, now were as small as goldfish scales, and surprisingly attractive.

This wasn't to say that Puck was any thing of beauty. Even though his horns and fangs had shrunk and his talons had rounded and flattened, his square-pupiled, goatish eyes still glowed with unmistakable Hellfire. And that face was never going to be anything but ugly.

Dan caught a flash of movement from his right and saw Meg following the waiter toward them. Meg was still dressed in work clothes—a linen suit, sensible shoes, and her briefcase.

She smiled at Dan and gave Puck a frankly curious stare as she joined them.

When the routines of introductions and ordering were out of the way, she turned to Dan. "I have several things to discuss with the two of you. I don't know much about your devil here, nor do I have any real idea of how likely his . . . rehabilitation . . . is going to be. None of that matters at the moment. Puck, I've spent much of my day on the phone with some of my colleagues at the ACLU. I did the preliminary work on the initiation of a class action antidiscrimination suit designed to force legislation mandating equal employment and housing opportunities for the Hellraised."

"She's talking about equal rights for devils," Puck said to Dan.

"I *know* what she's talking about. Shut up, already."

Meg glanced from the devil to Dan, a puzzled frown creasing her forehead. "But I don't know what *you're* talking about."

"Puck here used to be the guy in charge of translating clearly worded communications into High Bureaucratese. He's taken delight all day in translating bureaucratic babble-speak back into English for me, whether I needed it or not."

Meg said, "I thought my way of phrasing things was clear and to the point."

Dan kissed her. "I know, gorgeous. And that little touch of the delusional is part of your charm."

Meg laughed. "Fine. Let me tell you where I am in my . . . my quest for equal rights for the Hellraised. Was that clear enough?"

Dan nodded. So did Puck, who grinned when he did it.

Meg filled both of them in on her reasoning behind the need for such a class action suit, and finished with a shrug. "I don't have the manpower or the time to do this right. But a couple of old friends of mine who are still with the ACLU are going to take my preliminary work and build a case around it. If." She paused.

Dan watched Puck, who had been looking amused by the whole idea of human lawyers fighting for his sort.

Puck raised one scaly eyeridge and said, "If?"

"If you can convince your . . . your what? Associates? Friends?"

"Fellow damnedsouls," Puck suggested.

Meg pursed her lips. "Fellow damnedsouls. If you can persuade them to go into the offices of the ACLU around the state and make public statements about their grievances. The jobs they've tried to get, the housing they've been turned away from, the sorts of abuses that they've had to suffer."

Puck tipped his head to one side and thought about it for a moment. "I'm not actually on speaking terms with any of the other Hellraised at the moment. However, I imagine I could find a way to get in touch with a few who wouldn't hurt me too much—and they could pass the information on."

"Fine." Meg opened her briefcase, took several sheets of paper out of it, and passed them across to Puck. "Addresses of the offices statewide."

Puck smirked. "We knew where they were."

"Fine." Meg didn't react to the smirk or the implication.

Instead, she said, "The good news is, a successful suit will make life here easier for everyone, I think. The bad news is, it's a long-term project. In the meantime, we need to do something for your people *now*, before they have equal rights. And since I think it's likely that very few people will hire the Hellraised as things stand, I think we need to find a way for the Hellraised to employ themselves."

Puck nodded. "The higher-ups are pretty well taken care of in that regard. They have Satco—but unfortunately for most of the lower-echelon Hellspawn, Satco doesn't employ all of us. I don't think any company can claim to gainfully employ one hundred percent of an entire ethnic population in a state."

Dan snorted. "That does sound unlikely."

Meg said, "So what I need to know, Puck, is this: does anyone in your organization have any ideas for self-starting employment?"

Puck thought for a while. Dinner arrived while he sat there with his eyes tightly shut, his face screwed into an expression of extreme concentration. He didn't even notice the food.

Neither Dan nor Meg said anything. They waited, silently eating their Bean Burgers and Caesar salads.

Suddenly Puck's eyes opened. "I remember something. But it's something really, really big. It's not like vegetable stands or anything. Before his—disappearance—the first head of Satco, Agonostis, made plans for a big amusement park kind of thing, called Devil's Point. He intended it to be a place where Hellraised could operate a legitimate business. It would have been huge! Thousands, maybe tens of thousands, of us would have been required to run it." Puck briefly outlined what he recalled about the amusement park, and Dan found himself becoming interested.

"Could the Hellraised really do that—bring back extinct animals and showcase them in their natural habitats from the times when they lived?"

"I couldn't have, even when I had my powers, but the fallen angels could. That comes under the heading of a 'benign miracle'—as long as the dinosaurs and whatnot can't do any harm—and the Fallen can do any sort of benign miracle they like." Puck shook his head. "That park was a possibility once, but it isn't going to happen now."

"It sounds like it would work," Meg said. "What went wrong?"

"A couple of things. Scumslag, the new guy in charge of Satco, didn't come up with the plans, so rumor has it that he's dragging his heels in trying to implement them. That's the first problem, and for all I know, the scuttlebutt may have been wrong. I wasn't all that high on the food chain even before they kicked me out."

Meg shrugged. "That sounds like typical bureaucratic stupidity to me. I've known people who've deep-sixed terrific ideas because they couldn't take credit for them. So we'll assume for the time being that what you heard is right. We may face some resistance from the CEO of Satco. What else?"

"The Hellraised can't get the land. I know right after our management turnover, the devils who were on the team said they'd found the ideal site for the amusement park, but nobody will sell property on that scale to the Hellraised. I guess that kind of thing happens when your company gets a bad reputation for sticky contracts. The funny thing is, people are desperate to sell their property to get out of the state, but they still won't sell to my kind."

An idea occurred to Meg. "Where's the property?"

Puck said, "Down by the beach somewhere. I wasn't

on the Devil's Point development team, so I really don't know."

"Can you hook me up with someone who does?"

"I *know* someone who does. The problem is that she won't have anything to do with me. I'm poison for anybody's career right now."

"Could you tell me how to reach her?"

"Sure. Just don't tell her how you got her number." He gave Meg a phone number. "Her name is Glopsmear. Tell her you're calling in regards to Devil's Point."

Meg started to tuck the number into her briefcase.

Puck said, "Wait. Aren't you going to call her?"

"Right now?"

"Satco doesn't have to worry about paying overtime or things like that, and it doesn't pay any attention to the regulations for an eight- or twelve-hour day. Jobs there are twenty-four hours a day."

Meg looked at what remained of her burger, and Dan saw a flicker of regret that she wasn't going to be able to finish it while it was hot. Dan empathized—the food was some of the best he'd ever had. But she shrugged and bit the bullet. She leaned over and kissed him on the cheek. "I'll be right back."

When she was gone, Dan said, "You could have at least waited until after she finished dessert to tell her that."

"I got the impression time was of some importance to her." He took a huge bite of his Bean Burger.

Suddenly Dan realized that Puck had said he couldn't eat vegetable matter.

Incredible how fast he's changing, he thought.

He was still pondering that when Puck looked up, wide-eyed, and ran for the bathroom.

Chapter 20

Meg nearly hung up. She'd counted nineteen rings, and she didn't see any reason to keep trying—but of course that was the moment that the voice on the other end said, "Satco, General Projects Division."

"May I speak to Glopsmear, please."

"Speaking."

"My name is Meg Lerner. I'm a lawyer calling on behalf of a consortium that has heard about your Devil's Point project, and may be interested in investing."

From the other end of the phone, silence. Then, "Devil's Point? But that project is dead."

"You can't get the land. I know. But I think I may have a solution."

"A solution would be worth a lot to me right now." The voice on the other end held an edge of excitement.

"Then when can we meet?"

"Where are you?"

"In Raleigh."

"I mean right now."

"Oh." Meg paused, then told her the name of the restaurant.

"Give me five minutes."

Click.

Meg hurried back to the table. Puck was just sliding into the seat when she got there.

"What did she say?"

Meg smiled at him. "That she'll be here in five minutes. She sounded excited."

Puck's face went slack and looked frightened for a moment. Then he said, "You haven't seen excitement until you've seen what she would do if she ran into me. I'm going to go outside and sleep in the back of your car, Dan. Get me when you're through meeting."

"The door's locked."

"As if that would be a problem."

He reached over and shook Meg's hand. His palm was tremendously hot, his scaly skin not entirely unpleasant to the touch, though certainly odd. "It's been a pleasure. I hope we'll meet again."

"Of course we will," she said to his retreating back.

She turned to Dan, who didn't seem surprised by the devil's hasty retreat.

"He's had a lot of problems with his own kind as well as ours," Dan said. He looked like he intended to go into detail, but he didn't get the chance.

A curling cloud of sulphurous yellow smoke erupted from the center of the room, in between several tables of diners. As people began to shriek and stumble backward, a solid form developed in the center of the smoke cloud. Meg's first impressions were of tremendously long hair that swirled in a cloud of its own, of powerful shoulders, muscled thighs, and enormous, jutting breasts. Her second impression, as the smoke cleared, was of a face that would stop clocks and cause birth defects.

Into the stunned silence, Meg cleared her throat. "Over here," she said, and all the customers went from staring at the female devil to staring at her. She shifted in her seat, wishing that Glopsmear had chosen a less dramatic entrance.

The devil wore a nicely cut gray summer wool business suit with a high hemline and an elegantly draped red blouse and carried a slim, expensive briefcase. Meg felt a moment of envy over that briefcase, but it passed quickly. The envy over those breasts lasted longer. Even at her age, Meg found very little wonder in the Wonder Bra, and still remembered with some anguish her junior high days when the only thing that came between her and her Playtex Cross-Your-Heart was a pair of rolled sweatsocks. Such feelings of inferiority faded, but never entirely died.

On the other hand, she thought with some gratitude, she could look at her face in the mirror in the morning without screaming.

Glopsmear settled into the seat Puck had so recently occupied and sniffed. "I didn't realize they served the Hellspawn here," she said. She didn't have any scales. She looked, in fact, almost human, except for her pale, pale blue eyes, which had those square pupils, and for her mouth, which was twice as wide as any human mouth Meg had ever seen. The mouth seemed to split her face in two, and when she smiled, Meg got a look at teeth that would have sent an orthodontist screaming. Oddly, she reminded Meg of Puck, but not in any way that Meg could put a finger on.

Meg shrugged. "Policies change."

"Indeed they do." The devil opened her briefcase and from it extracted a blue folder about an inch thick and several reduced-size copies of blueprints. "And if we could just get this project off the ground . . ."

Meg and Dan listened in amazement as Glopsmear took them over the planned Devil's Point Amusement Park. Meg studied the list of planned attractions, and realized that nowhere else in the world was there anything similar to even one of them. Devil's Point would be unique, educational, fascinating, fun . . . and it could be the first real draw to turn around North Carolina's ailing economy.

When Glopsmear got to the planned construction details, Meg and Dan looked at each other. "They're going to have to hire human construction companies to do this," Dan whispered.

"And humans who run hotels in the area are going to rack up." Meg considered the influx of international scholars who were going to want to use the library—every book ever written in *any* language; the paleontologists who would move into the prehistoric areas; the historians who would be able to talk with Julius Caesar and Hannibal and Hammurabi and Queen Elizabeth I in person. And the everyday people who would go there to play. To have fun. To get the bodies they'd always dreamed of.

I might do that, Meg thought. I could. *Real* perfect breasts. Not implants.

She said, "Once we acquire the land and construction starts, you folks might want to consider opening up the company and offering stock."

The devil said, "The problem is the land." She pulled out a plat map of part of Pender County. "This is the piece of ground we want. It's roughly ten miles by ten miles square, and we need all of it, of course. You can see that we've planned to utilize every square inch of the space. There are a few people who live there—we think they'd be amenable to selling. Our big problem comes from the owners of this stretch of land from here—" One talon dragged along a shaded area. "—to here. This is owned by people who aren't interesting in selling at any price."

"Then they're the only people in the state who aren't trying to get rid of property right now. Who are they?"

"You've heard of Forever Wilderness, Inc.?"

Meg felt her stomach knot. "The private company that buys up little parcels of land and acts like it's saving the universe. I sent them a thirty-dollar donation once and within the year received over two hundred dollars worth of mailings soliciting more money. They have great memes, but their corporate raison d'être is simply the propagation of their organization."

"So you have met."

Dan raised an eyebrow. "I donate to them."

Meg said, "I'll put garlic around your neck and give you a silver cross to ward them off. They're money vampires."

The devil laughed. "However, they really don't ever give up a piece of ground they've acquired, and they certainly weren't interested in selling to us, no matter how much our project might help the economy."

"Maybe we can work out a barter deal with them. Other land in the state is certainly up for grabs. How much are you willing to pay for the land if my consortium can get it for you?"

"You'll like this," the devil said. "Money is no object. We just want the land."

"Do you have the money now?"

"Our corporate war chest is very, very deep. The answer is yes. Whatever you have to pay to get the land, pay it, and we'll make the deal extremely profitable for you."

Meg reached out a hand and shook with Glopsmear. "When we're ready to do the deal, I'll let you know and we can work out the details then." She looked at the Devil's Point plans. "Would you mind if I took those with me to show to my investors? I think we're much more likely to get total cooperation from the group if they can see what a marvelous project this is."

Glopsmear smiled. Unfortunate, really. It looked like she'd tried to swallow a dinner plate and the plate had gotten stuck halfway down. "Take whatever you need. You know where to reach me."

"You'll be hearing from me soon."

The devil disappeared in another cloud of sulphur, and Meg twisted around in her seat and hugged Dan. "This could save North Carolina," she said.

Dan nodded. "It could. And if we could tie it in with the Great Devil Makeover as one example of the benefits our state will reap from taking advantage of the presence of the Hellraised, North Carolinians should be willing to support it."

"A lot of our success in doing that will depend on how well Puck does," Meg said.

Dan nodded, his expression becoming thoughtful. "If Puck can walk away from Hell and evil, that will make all the difference in the world."

Chapter 21

Dan put his key into the lock and paused.

I forgot about the imp, he thought. It's been in there all day. God only knows what kind of mess it's made.

He took a deep breath. How much worse could it be than when he left? Well, he could have stuff dripping off the ceiling in the rest of the apartment. Everything he owned might be shredded and in piles. All the dishes might be broken. He opened the door and his first thought was that he'd been robbed. Then he realized someone had just cleaned up. He heard off-key humming, and after a moment he realized the song was "Copacabana."

Why would anyone hum "Copacabana"?

He stepped inside, switched on the light, and tried to get over the shock.

The previously grimy upholstery looked brand new—the worn spots no longer showed, the blue-and-brown herringbone had returned, and the overall pallor of *gray* no longer existed. But that was the least of the apartment's changes. He felt the next one under his feet, where carpet that had been pounded into a flat, felted mass now sprang up beneath his shoes. He slipped the shoes off and sank into the delightful cushiony resistance of new carpet. "How did he replace the carpet?" Dan asked Puck.

"Fetch is an it. And it didn't replace the carpet. It rugged it—went through and twisted all the fibers back into yarn." Puck, standing just to the left of Dan, bent down and experimentally twisted one of the strands. "It could have gotten them tighter. If we were back in Hell . . ."

The carpet wasn't splotchy neutral beige with darker stains anymore, either. It had become a solid, pleasant shade of light blue, and its color no longer matched that of the cigarette-smoke-stained walls. Now that Dan looked at them, the walls weren't the dingy yellow-brown that they'd been when he left that morning. They were white, that sort of snowfield-in-sunlight white designers so admired.

The kitchen wasn't covered in Jackson Pollock food splatters anymore, either. Its white-on-white brilliance matched the living room's . . . and the floor glistened. My landlady is going to *love* me, he thought.

"Fetch did all of this?"

"Imps have their uses. Takes time to train them, but it pays off. Of course, every now and then you get hungry and forget yourself. Then you have to start all over again with another one."

"You eat imps?"

"All Hellraised are cannibals. Didn't you know that? It's not like you can grow food in Hell. We're the only living things there. You don't see that sort of cannibalism dirtside, though. The little bastards are too expensive to eat. A colleague of mine fried up a couple of gargoyles and a six-pack of imps for a midnight snack, because he didn't know we had to pay for their replacement bodies, and the bill from Hell was so steep he couldn't pay it. He got recalled."

That entire revelation fell into the category of things Dan didn't want to know about the Hellraised. He didn't comment on it. Instead, he sneaked the imp a Mr. Goodbar for doing such a good job and gave him a quick scratch behind the ears. Then he checked his answering machine. Three messages.

Beep!

"Phone tag! You're it! Call me! Bye!"

Dan wondered if his sister ever visited her home for more than five minutes. This is long past absurd, he thought.

Beep!

"Hello, Dan, it's Janna. I'm sorry I got so upset about Bits. It isn't like the Hellspawn haven't been chowing down on family pets since they arrived. I should have kept him out of the way. Anyway, I'd still like to help out with your project . . . and I'd still like to see you, too. Call me when you can."

Beep!

"Hi, Dan. Meg here. Just wanted to say I enjoyed our dinner date, and my uncle is so excited about the plans I took home he's called his investors and they're meeting him in the bank tomorrow morning. I think this is going to work. I still want to find some time for just the two of us. See you tomorrow to let you know how things went."

He went into the kitchen to get himself a Coke, and the smell hit him. An underlying ammonia clean with an overlay of the lemony scent of floor polish. And a touch of cinnamon.

The scents were like a gut punch. He hadn't smelled them together since the days and nights when he could still come home to Francie.

Francie had died in Colorado. Her body was there. The house Dan had shared with her was there. His past, his life—they were in Colorado, too. She had never seen this apartment, and yet suddenly her presence filled the kitchen for him as completely as if she had spent her entire life in it with him. His eyes filled with tears and he leaned against the refrigerator, waiting for the pain to pass.

It didn't.

After the last horrible year, when she'd wasted and faded and suffered pain that only drugs and unconsciousness could lessen, he'd thought her final release into death would be a relief. He thought that he could stand her absence and his loss, knowing that she no longer suffered. He had been calm at her funeral. It was for the best. For the best.

But his pain after her death had worsened. Every day, something happened that he wanted to tell Francie. Every time he turned around, she wasn't there. Every time he rolled over in bed and reached for her in his sleep, his arm touched an emptiness so terrible it burned. Her presence had filled his life, but her absence filled it more.

The new job, the new apartment, the return to his home state—he sought them out to flee the yawning void of Francie that threatened to swallow him up. He rebuilt himself around a life that had never known her, and tucked his hollow soul away with the pain, pretending she and her love and those few perfect years before the cancer came had never existed.

He pushed himself upright, wiped his eyes, got his Coke from the fridge with jaw-clenched determination, and returned to the living room.

He sprawled into his recliner and stared at the ceiling while Puck channel surfed.

"Dan?"

"Yeah?"

"Can I ask you a question?"

"Go ahead."

The devil turned to face him. "It's none of my business; I'm just curious. You don't seem like the two-timing type. So why?"

Dan closed his eyes. "You're right. It isn't any of your business."

"Touchy."

Dan popped the top on his Coke and took a swallow.

Puck watched. "How'd you meet them?"

Dan said nothing.

"Look, you like them. They both like you. Nothing wrong with that. But sneaking around boffing two women at the same time has been known to get men into more trouble than they ever imagined."

"I interviewed them on my show, both in the same week. I asked them out. They accepted."

They were supposed to take away the pain. They were supposed to make him forget that other life . . . that other, perfect, irretrievable time. But he'd been kidding himself. They couldn't replace Francie, and they couldn't make him forget her, and they couldn't take away his pain.

"You fool around with women," Puck said, "they'll break your heart."

Dan looked at him, but did not say what he was thinking.

You can't break what's already broken.

Chapter 22

THURSDAY, JUNE 9TH

Dan got himself up at four the next morning so he would have some time to himself before the day started. He fixed himself a bowl of cereal—when did they stop calling them *Sugar* Frosted Flakes?—and ate his breakfast in bed while watching *Headline News* on CNN. The damned human race kept itself busy with the business of human damnation—fighting in the Middle East, war in Eastern Europe, war in Africa; torture in Central America; rape, murder, thievery, violence, hatred and greed everywhere. The reporters dished out their morning dose of poison with the unemotional voices and blank-faced "we're objective" expressions that said, Not me. I am above this. I am pure of the taint of human pain and misery.

"Fuck you," he yelled at them. "You're human! Give a shit about humans, you bastards."

He punched the off button on the controller and threw it across the room. In the shower, he stood under a spray of icy water until he had his anger under control, then dressed and went into the living room to wake Puck.

The devil slept on the couch, curled into a ball, snoring softly.

"Puck," Dan said. "Wake up."

"Mmmrmph?"

"Wake up. C'mon. Wake up. We have a lot to do today."

"We . . . do? What?"

"*I* have to go to work. Janna's going to go with you while your suits are fitted. Then you need to meet with more advertisers and do a couple of spots for the promotions for the advertisers we already have. I think she'll probably stick around with you for that. When the two of you are done, you're probably going to have to talk with Meg's investment group. After you've done that, you and I need to set up a schedule for on-site promotions and work out your calendar."

"Oh." The devil gave a tremendous sigh, rolled over, and shoved his face into the couch back.

Dan flipped on the light. The devil groaned, rolled back over, and swung his legs to the floor. "You'll survive—" Dan started to say, but when he got a good look at Puck, words left him. Puck's scales had shrunk to the size of pinheads, and their hard new-penny gleam had dulled and softened. Puck's hide could almost be mistaken for skin—in fact, Dan had seen rich women come back from the Riviera with skin browner and leatherier than his, though without the slight metallic underlay that made him look like he'd had a good paint job.

His face was another wonder. The horns, shrunken to the buttons that would look at home on the forehead of a baby goat, almost disappeared beneath a fuzzy thatch of soft, black hair. The fangs, shorter—almost but not quite the length of human canines—no longer bulged outward or forced Puck's mouth into a perpetual sneer. Without that sneering expression, he looked somehow vulnerable. His eyes, with their square pupils and pale irises, still clearly marked his Hellish origins. The expression in them, though, was neither scornful nor hateful, but full of wonder.

Puck sat staring at his outstretched hands. The talons were gone entirely, Dan saw, replaced by thick, rather ugly—but human-looking—nails. A few curling black hairs grew out from between the scales on Puck's forearms and the backs of his hands.

"I've changed," Puck whispered.

Dan could only nod.

"I did kind things for people . . . yesterday . . . did those things because I . . . because I wanted to. I *wanted* to."

"You haven't had the chance to do things you wanted very often, have you?"

Puck glanced up at him. "Hell is not noted for its enthusiastic support of personal choice."

"No. I don't suppose it is."

"Look at me. I remember hands like these."

"You're starting to remember your past?"

"Maybe. I can't be sure. But last night, Dan, something happened to me that . . ." He shook his head and stared off into space. "I dreamed, Dan. I *dreamed*."

Dan gave him an encouraging smile. "You dreamed something special?"

For a moment, Puck looked impatient. "I don't know what I dreamed . . . it doesn't matter what I dreamed. The dreaming is the thing." Dan thought he saw the beginnings of tears forming in the corners of the devil's eyes. "There are no dreams in Hell. There are only nightmares."

Chapter 23

"Gunga Dan, you're on the air."

"Those Hellraised monsters ate my sweet little doggie Fifi, and I want them to rot in Hell forever."

"Talk about redundant." <click> "WKTU, you're on the air. Go ahead, caller."

"We can't give the Hellraised rights, Dan. We can't hire them. They'll fill all the minimum-wage jobs and leave the poor without any way to make a living."

"I had the Hellraised figured for middle management, myself." <click> "Gunga Dan, you're on the air."

"You are a blasphemer and an iniquitous hellbound fiend and we're going to get you."

"We're living in the age of enlightenment today." <click> "Hi. You're on the air. Try to say something sensible."

"Dan?"

"Ye-e-e-e-sss?"

"I just wanted to thank you for what you're trying to do. Even if it doesn't work, I think the fact that you're doing your part to give the Hellraised a second chance is wonderful. I don't want to think of anyone being tortured in Hell forever, and I hope your Great Devil Makeover works."

Dan was silent for an instant. Then he said, "I know exactly what you mean. Thanks for calling."

All morning, the calls kept coming in. The callers expressed hope, swore and threatened, shouted, laughed, told stories of experiences they'd had with the Hellraised, talked about loved ones dead and gone who'd led less-than-exemplary lives.

The minister of a local church called in and said that he and his parishioners, heartened by WKTU's attempt to make North Carolina a place people would want to live again, were following the radio station's example and adopting the two gargoyles that had been hanging around the church grounds. Further, he said, he wanted to challenge other churches to find their own Hellraised souls and do what they could to turn them around.

Dan raised a triumphant fist and Darlene, sitting at her desk near the main door, grinned at him and mouthed the words "Way to go."

A boy from one of NC State's fraternities called in to say that he and his frat brothers were so inspired by the Great Devil Makeover that they were going to go out and find a succubus and attempt to rehabilitate her and that they challenged other fraternities to do the same. Dan winced, and started adding a disclaimer every ten or fifteen minutes reminding listeners that the radio station could not guarantee the safety of the Great Devil Makeover project and advised others to follow caution and common sense if following its example.

His warnings didn't seem to slow anyone down. Sororities began calling in to say they'd found imps and gargoyles and were adopting them. Churches called in to respond to the challenge the first church had raised. A local chapter of the Girl Scouts adopted a swarm of gremlins, and the Raleigh branch of the Daughters of the Confederacy decided to make a project out of a fallen angel.

Every once in a while, someone would call in to tell

Dan he was leading Raleigh into perdition. Dan cheerfully told those callers Raleigh was right in the middle of perdition and he was just trying to dig it out.

By the time Sandy came in, she had to fight her way through a picket line of Mothers Against Unchained Devils and elbow her way past a thicket of television cameras from stations in Charlotte, High Point, Fayetteville, and Wilmington.

"Oh, babe, it's Hell out there," she said and grinned.

Dan leaned back in his chair, enjoying the silence while the advertisements ran, and grinned back at her. "They're listening," he said.

"Are they ever." Sandy flopped into her own seat and took a sip of her coffee. "Somebody's draped banners across the street that say, 'Home of the Great Devil Makeover' and 'WKTU Believes' and 'St. Dan for President' and . . . I don't know. Three or four other ones. M.A.U.D. is raising hell—they'll probably rip your clothes off when you go through the picket line."

"Maybe I'll go out the back door."

She raised an eyebrow. "That would be chickenshit of you. Your public awaits. Christ, I had people asking for *my* autograph as I was coming through the door, just because I work here. You gotta go through the front door, babe. They love you out there."

"Except for M.A.U.D."

Sandy pointed her index finger at him and fired an imaginary pistol. "You can handle the mommies. Go get 'em, Tex."

Chapter 24

Lucifer towered over Scumslag, radiating black flames and fury. "I thought you had things under control up there. I thought you were going to get the Devil's Point project online and increase my net in damnedsouls and cash. I *didn't* expect you to permit a situation to develop in which my fodder was actively trying to convert my employees."

Scumslag grinned at him, unshaken. "Your Reeking Foulness, this plays into our hands. Which of the Hellraised do you think these humans have managed to catch?"

Lucifer said nothing.

"The ones I sent out there for them to catch, Your Awfulness. Every single one of our participants has a special mission—to see to the individual temptation and damnation of the person or persons who try to subvert him to the side of goodness." His grin grew broader. "Just think how much more we can do to them when they trust us, O Father of Lies. Think about how vulnerable they become when they welcome us into their homes and their lives, when they pity us, when they care about what happens to us."

Lucifer arched an eyebrow and cut off the special effects. That black flame took a lot of energy. "So you planned this?"

"Well, no . . . but I know how to take advantage of a situation when I find one."

"So this is . . ."

"Serendipity, I like to think."

Lucifer studied the devil. "I'm inclined to give you enough rope to hang yourself, Scumslag. We can both take as a given the fact that if any of the Hellraised you've assigned to this project go over to the other side, I'll take it out of your hide. At the very *least*, I'll take it out of your hide. You should probably consider your fate to be less pleasant than that, if any of my little sinners should be so weak as to have a change of heart."

Lucifer stretched his wings as he said that, and let his eyes glow red, and caused lightning to flash around his head, and made Hell tremble and crack.

Scumslag, oblivious to the artistry of Lucifer's presentation, just bobbed his head like the small-town businessman he'd once been and said, "I understand, sir. And you can count on me."

Chapter 25

Dan picked up Puck and Fetch from the bank, got a report from Meg on the success of the meeting, gave her a quick kiss in passing, and left with devil and imp in tow. Puck had changed since morning. He had no horns at all, and his skin was beginning to smooth out. Now he looked like he'd had bad acne when he was younger, but not like he'd had scales the size of quarters the day before.

The devil said, "What else do we have today?"

"We don't. You've cut your spots and finished up the meeting, and those were the last two things on the agenda. How are you feeling?"

The devil smiled and Dan saw genuine warmth in the smile. "Almost human again."

Dan let them into his apartment and almost jumped out of his skin when he realized they weren't alone in there.

His sister, sitting in his recliner, looked up from a copy of Jonathan Kellerman's *Devil's Waltz*. She held up the book and grinned. "Amazing how tempting these titles get if you live in North Carolina." She put the book down and got up. "I've been waiting for you."

"Did the landlady let you in?"

"Of course not. You gave me an extra set the last time you locked yourself out. Remember?"

"Nope. I forgot." He looked around for his niece. "Where's Amy?"

"With Mom." She glanced at Puck and a flash of puzzlement crossed her face. With a tentative smile, she said, "Hi. I'm Cynthia, Dan's sister."

"Puck," the devil said. "Dan's experiment. And Fetch is . . . Dan, where's Fetch?"

Dan looked around. "I thought he was with you."

Puck frowned. "I smell . . . dog," he said, and Dan said, "Oh, no. My landlady had her door open when we came past." He flung the door open and ran out onto the landing, then plunged down the first flight of stairs, and careened into Mrs. Carte as she stood talking to her across-the-landing neighbor. "Your dog," he panted, and then the yipping started. And stopped.

Fetch shot out of the doorway, his throat bulging, and launched himself upstairs.

"Spit it out!" Dan shouted, and took off after him.

"Poop-sie!" Mrs. Carte wailed, and came thundering up the metal stairs behind him. Dan could see his rent going up with every step the imp took.

Puck, almost indistinguishable from a human, knelt by the imp, holding him upside-down. "Spit . . . it . . . out!" he said.

The imp opened its mouth and a battered, sodden, disgusting piece of dog fell out.

"Too late," Dan said, looking away.

"Poopsie!" Mrs. Carte squealed, and the dog piece yipped.

Dan turned to look. It wasn't just a piece of the dog. It was the whole dog, and it seemed to be fine. *Swallow it again, Fetch,* he thought, but he said, "Is he okay?"

"Oh, poor widdle Poopsie, that mean ol' imp didn't eat you." She was holding the soggy rat and crooning at it; to Dan, the dog looked humiliated to be seen with its mistress. Dan sympathized. He had the sudden urge to see Fetch eat Mrs. Carte.

She turned to Puck. "Thank you for saving my little doggie for me. My poor widdle Poopsie," she added in an aside to the dog. Then she moved up to Puck, her wide hips swinging, her eyelashes batting. "If there's ever anything I can do for you . . ." She smiled, and Dan shivered.

Puck managed a polite nod. "I'll keep that in mind." He took a step back from her, and another, and a third. Dan though he saw a flash of cold fear in the devil's eyes. He understood. Mrs. Carte in amorous mode scared the bejeezus out of him, too. They hurried back into his apartment, this time with Fetch in tow. Dan closed and locked the door and leaned against it. "Sorry, Cyn. Things have been kind of unsettled lately."

Cyn nodded. "I can see that." She turned her attention to the devil. "You're Puck. The one I've been hearing about on the radio? But you don't look like a devil."

"He's changed," Dan said.

"I've changed." Puck shook his head, his bemusement apparent in his cockeyed smile. "I can't believe how much I've changed."

Cyn walked over to him, held out her hand, and when he shook it, said, "Good luck, Puck. I've been rooting for you."

Dan hugged his sister. "Did you know it's generally considered tacky to break into people's houses? I should have you arrested."

She laughed. "And you know what? When I walked in here, I thought I really had broken in to a stranger's home. This is your place? I almost turned back around and walked out."

"Thanks a lot. It wasn't that bad before."

"Maybe not, but it's never been this good. And when

did you get new carpet? And how did you talk that termagant into springing for that . . . and new paint?"

"Imps could put professional cleaners out of business," Dan said. "The carpet and paint are the same as the last time you were here. The imp just cleaned and fixed them."

Cynthia looked around the room, slowly taking in the changes. "How much does he charge? Amy crayoned all over her bedroom wall and in spite of 'Hints from Heloise' and an entire library of 'You-Too-Can-Have-A-Spotless-House' books, I can't get those marks off."

"I'll bring him by," Puck said. "I need to keep him in shape."

Dan stuck his hands in his pockets and studied his sister. "I can't believe you just dropped by for a visit without any ulterior motive."

"*Moi*?" She made innocent eyes at him.

"*Vous*."

She sighed. "Would you believe that I came over to harass you further about attending Amy's party?"

"No."

"You're entirely too smart to be an older brother." She shrugged and the grin on her face vanished. "I'm worried about Mom and Dad."

Dan's neck tensed. "Mom was in a great mood the last time I talked to her. And I'm sure Arthur will be fine."

"Probably. If he can survive you, he can deal with anything."

"What's that supposed to mean?"

"Oh, come on! You've been a pain to Dad ever since he and Mom got married. I think you got your nose out of joint when he took your place as the man of the house."

Dan arched an eyebrow at her. "You become a

therapist when I wasn't looking?" He saw her expression darken, though, and backed off. "Sorry. Why are you more worried now than yesterday?"

"Dad said the president of Daltech stopped by this morning to talk to him, for no particular reason. He got the feeling that he's next on the list to go."

"He thinks they're looking at him?"

"Yes."

Dan nodded. "Even if he loses his job, they'll be okay until he finds something else. They've been smart with their money. They have an IRA. They've been putting ten percent of every paycheck he gets into no-load mutual funds, and they've been reinvesting the dividends. It would hurt their retirement fund some if they had to use part of that money now, but probably not all that much."

"I didn't come for the Wall Street update," she said. She looked up at him, eyes concerned. "I think they could stand to know that you're worried about them, too. Both of them. Not just Mom."

Dan nodded. She was right. He didn't need to stay away when Arthur was home. He needed to go by and visit and let them know he would do whatever he could to help out. His differences with Arthur—and Arthur's differences with him—would have to disappear. At least for a while. "I'll find some time to stop by."

"Do it before he loses his job."

"I know. I will."

Chapter 26

FRIDAY, JUNE 10TH

Darlene waved Dan to a stop as he was on his way out of the studio the next afternoon.

"What's up?"

Darlene grinned and handed him a stack of front pages. "I like the ones of Puck with the actress," she said. "Look."

The pictures flattered Janna, and Janna's presence did a lot to make Puck more palatable. Puck trying on clothes, Puck standing in a bakery, Puck grinning in a barber's chair—all of those became slightly more newsworthy, and considerably more front pageworthy, with beautiful, smiling Janna at his side.

"How did you get her involved in this?" Darlene asked.

Dan didn't bother to mention that the two of them were dating. He just smiled and said, "Actually, she called me."

"Ooh-la-la."

"They're good pictures," he said.

"You can keep them. We have quite a stack. *Charlotte News and Observer* did the biggest story." She smiled an evil smile. "But they spelled your name wrong."

He started to take the front pages, but she said, "Don't go yet. That's not all." She lugged a mail sack out from under her desk. "You have fans," she said. "I'd be careful opening the ones addressed to 'Asshole, WKTU.' "

Dan raised an eyebrow. "Those would be for Bernie." He paused. "There really are letters to Asshole?"

"If you don't believe me, see for yourself."

Dan reached in and fished out a handful of letters. Some had return addresses, some didn't. The ones that didn't, he realized quickly, tended to be addressed to "The Human Hellspawn" or "Devil Dan" or, as Darlene had said, just "Asshole." He dropped the handful of letters back in the bag and frowned. "I can't believe the post office delivered those."

"It isn't their job to censor your mail for you. For all the post office knows, you had your name legally changed to Asshole. I mean, people have done stupider things." She gave him a saccharine smile and went back to her desk.

"Thanks, Darlene. Your support means so much."

She laughed and winked at him.

The weather had turned horrendous. The temperature on the bank sign read 104.3, and with the high humidity, it felt like twice that. A mad sun beat down out of a white-hot, merciless sky in which not even the smallest of clouds survived, and it melted tar on the road and set up shimmering mirages that reflected from the pavement, from the trunks of cars ahead of him in traffic, from sidewalks. The air conditioner in the Mustang wasn't working, and driving with the windows open felt like sitting in front of a blast furnace.

When he got home, he found Meg in her car, which she'd parked under a cluster of dogwoods. She had the seat tilted back, eyes closed, air conditioner running. He rapped on the window.

She opened her eyes and smiled at him. She had a pretty smile. It lighted up her ordinary face, and made her almost radiant. She swung the car door open and slid out. "Hi, you."

"Hi, yourself. You take off early?"

"I figured that since I had good news, I should. Besides, today was a slow day. I only had two clients scheduled and one of them canceled out on me at the last minute. She decided she didn't want that divorce after all, I guess."

Dan picked her up and swung her around, hugging her close to his chest as he did. Their skin stuck, their damp clothes clung to themselves and each other, and their foreheads and upper lips beaded with sweat. Meg laughed. Dan liked her laugh. It had just a hint of looniness, and there was nothing artful or artificial about it. Her laugh was rather like the rest of Meg, in fact.

He put her down. "So what's your good news?"

"Two things. The ACLU has decided to go ahead with the antidiscrimination suit for the Hellraised. My friend at the office called me today; she told me not to expect quick results, of course."

"Of course. That's terrific. And the second thing?"

"The consortium has reviewed the Devil's Point plan and has agreed that it's a worthwhile project, and they've met with representatives from Satco, and have already negotiated a deal whereby they purchase the land with Satco's money and for their work they'll not only get a handsome immediate return but stock and shares in Devil's Point itself." Meg made a little face at that. "I have to say that I didn't care much for the attitude of the fallen angels and devils who did the negotiating. And they came with so many of their own lawyers . . ." Her gaze took on a faraway look for an instant, and she shivered. "There but for the grace of God . . ." she said.

"Not so," he said. "Those weren't people who ended

up in Hell accidentally, and they aren't people who would have to stay there. They have a choice—they are where they choose to be. People consciously choose evil in their lives—their crummy childhoods and evil parents don't make them evil. They, and you and I, become what we wish to be."

Meg looked up at him. "That's an odd attitude for someone who's trying to help the Hellraised out of Hell."

"I think you can show people that life can be different than it is, and that it can be better, but you can't make their decisions for them."

Meg stood on tiptoe and kissed him on the cheek. "You're probably right."

"I'm certainly right." He looked down at Meg and frowned. He was forgetting something. "Oh. Shit. My mail. I've got to get my mail."

"I came to get my *male*," Meg said, giving his shirt a little tug, "and since Puck and his friend are still tied up with the consortium, I'd like to see if I could tempt you upstairs for just a . . . quickie."

Francie tugged at Dan's mind, but he forced himself to not think about her. He said, "By all means. Tempt away. But would you mind tempting me someplace that isn't so frigging humid?"

They ran up the stairs together, hand in hand.

When the explosion blew in Dan's bedroom window an hour later, luck alone saved them from serious injury. Meg, in the windowless bathroom washing up, missed everything but the noise and the pressure that blew the bathroom door open. Dan, with a bad case of postcoital munchies, had been standing in the kitchen going through the freezer and trying to find any sort of ice cream that the damned devil hadn't scarfed. The boxes of Drumsticks and Frosty-Pops and cartons of chocolate and vanilla ice cream (Dan refused to buy anything with a stupid name like Cookie Dough Crunch on general principle) were still in the freezer, but all of them were empty. He'd just finished wishing the devil back into Hell when the earth shook, glass shattered, and a roar like a freight train erased the mundane sounds of life as it had been.

In the bathroom, Meg screamed. He ran to help, but stopped as soon as he opened his bedroom door. The floor glittered with knives of glass. The waterbed sparkled, and thin sprays of water shot straight into the air from the places where tiny glass spears stuck through the sheet and into the vinyl.

He looked around for something to put on his feet, raced back to the entryway closet, and pulled out a pair of sneakers. Then he ran across the bedroom floor and skidded to a halt in the master bathroom doorway. Meg crouched in the still-full tub, her arms over her head. "Meg! Are you okay?"

"What was that?"

"I don't know yet, but it threw glass all across the room and punched holes in the bed. If we'd still been in it, it would have punched holes in us, too."

Meg stared up at him. "What *happened*?"

Dan shrugged. "Don't know. Stay there. I'll get you some clothes and shoes from my closet. Your stuff is covered in glass."

He got her a T-shirt and some sweatpants and another pair of his sneakers. When she'd dressed, she looked like a little kid playing dress-up in her father's clothes. Dan put on underwear, jeans and a T-shirt, too. Then the two of them crept to the window, keeping low in case whatever had caused the destruction wasn't done yet.

"Oh, shit," he whispered. "My *car*!"

Parts of the Mustang still burned. Flames shot out of the windows from the charred interior. One door lay on the grass quadrant between two apartment buildings, and the other hung canted on broken hinges. A snow flurry of paper turned the ground white for a hundred yards in all directions. People were running everywhere.

"Where did all the paper come from?" he wondered, and as soon as he did, he knew. "Someone tried to kill me," he said. He stared at Meg. "Someone tried to *kill* me! Someone mailed me a bomb. He wanted to . . ."

Dan felt light-headed. Queasy. He couldn't seem to catch his breath, and his lips began to tingle. The room spun, and at that moment Meg said, "Oh, no you don't." She grabbed his arm and dragged him out to the couch and made him sit with his head between his legs until he could breathe again.

By that time, Dan could hear the sirens in the distance. He stood, still feeling weak and sick, and told Meg, "Let's go. We need to tell someone what happened. And we need to see if anyone else is hurt."

He ran out his door and down the stairs. The stink of acrid, synthetic-scented smoke filled his lungs and burned his eyes. He coughed and kept going; he saw a knot of people clustered near his car and felt a sudden sick dread. Someone had been hurt. Someone had been killed by the blast, shattered, splattered across cars and concrete, torn, hurled down . . .

He pushed his way through the people, found a man kneeling in the center of the circle, and he realized his worst fears were true. A woman lay, bloody, shredded, unbreathing, while the man did CPR. Filling the lungs with air, pressing on the chest.

Dead because of me, Dan thought. Dead because I brought this danger here.

The ambulance pulled into the parking lot and its lights, flashing red and white, cast shadows in daylight. The paramedics swung out of their front doors, ran to the back, and a second later forced their way through the crowd, pushing a stretcher with a box of supplies on top. A young woman with pale hair, broad shoulders, a narrow waist, mid-twenties, confident swagger; an equally young man, blank-eyed as a war veteran coming up out of the trenches. They knelt by the man doing CPR. Dan couldn't hear what they said, but the man nodded and moved back. The ambulance's EMT team checked the victim's pulse and looked for breathing. The female rescuer took a tube and a metal cylinder and pried the woman's jaws open and slid the tube down her throat. The other rescuer had cut through her shirt and was attaching sticky circles to her chest and hooking them up to some sort of heart monitor. Police arrived and started clearing the bystanders, and the man who'd done the initial rescuing stood and backed away with the crowd. His blood-smeared face and hands made him look like another victim. Dan started to work his way toward the other man, when the man glanced over at Dan and smiled a weary, sad smile. Dan looked into his eyes and froze at what he saw.

Pale yellow-gold eyes. Square pupils.

Puck.

Chapter 27

Janna got home from another long day with Puck and called her agent, Kate Matorsi, to see if she'd heard anything about the part she'd read for.

"You aren't going to be happy."

"They don't want me."

"No. Sorry, Janna. The director wanted someone with a bit more visibility. They went with someone out of California."

She stared up at her ceiling and counted to ten. "Okay. Fine. You've been saying 'Establish yourself in a regional market and have an impeccable record.' Well, I have a great record—and it isn't doing me a goddamn bit of good."

"You aren't going to get every part you want."

"Maybe not. But I should be able to expect better than this sort of response. Not even a thank you for coming in to read? Not even a personal call telling me they'd chosen someone else?"

Kate sighed. "They were doing you a favor, Janna—not the other way around. Did you send them a note thanking them for their time?"

Janna rolled her eyes, but changed her voice to one that would sound chagrined. "Oh. I hadn't thought of that."

"Think of it," Kate said. "If you don't stand out as

someone who is thoughtful, professional, and pleasant to work with, people won't want to work with you, no matter how talented you are—because the field is full of talented people who *are* thoughtful, professional, and pleasant to work with."

Janna put a smile on her face, because she'd heard people could tell if the person on the other end of the phone was smiling from the sound of her voice. She said, "You always give me such good advice, Kate. I'll write them a note now."

She hung up the phone and muttered, "And when I make it big, they can kiss my ass and beg for every single thing they want."

Someone rang her doorbell.

She wasn't expecting company, and the men she dated knew they were never to stop by without calling first. Paul didn't listen too well, though, or he thought the thousand or so dollars he left on the counter for her every couple of weeks "to help out" bought him special privileges. If he were standing out there, she wanted to have a good excuse why she couldn't see him. She didn't want company.

But when she looked through the peephole, it wasn't Paul after all, but the devil Puck—the new, almost human Puck. Neatly dressed in a polo shirt and Sans-A-Belt slacks and tasseled loafers, looking very much like a golfer on his way to the links for a few holes after work. A golfing devil; that image wasn't nearly as jarring as it seemed it ought to have been. He carried a small wicker picnic basket with a large blue bow on the handle.

She opened the door and studied the basket for an instant, then said, "Hi."

"Hello. I'm sure you've seen about enough of me today, what with the photo shoots and the reporters and everything, so I won't take much of your time. I brought something for you." He held the basket out for her.

She took it, and felt the contents shift when she did. She lifted the cover, and a gorgeous Himalayan kitten stared back at her out of eyes as deeply blue as an October sky.

She studied the kitten, which was undeniably cute, then glanced over at Puck. He stood at her doorway smiling nervously. "I'm really sorry I ate your dog. I hope you like her—I mean the kitten . . . I didn't actually know if you liked cats, you know, but I thought she was rather elegant, you know, like you, and at the same time very . . ." He blushed. "Very pretty. So I really do hope you like her."

I can charm a devil to speechlessness, but I can't convince a couple of film assholes to cast me in a part I want. Well . . . I've heard that devils have their uses, too. Not this one, maybe—but he ought to have friends.

"It's beautiful," she said. The kitten crawled out of the basket and up her arm, tiny claws digging into her skin and catching in the cotton of her shirt. When it reached her shoulder, it attached itself firmly with those claws and began to butt the side of her face with its head.

Puck smiled. "I'm glad you like her."

"I do. Thank you so much." She paused, thoughtful. "Would you like to come in for a moment? You said you were on your way home, but . . ."

"I left Fetch down in the car. It won't get too hot for him in there, no matter how hot it gets . . . but I don't want him to be bored."

"You got a car since this morning?"

"After you left, the Chevy dealer supplied me with a nice Blazer. They thought it was sort of appropriate."

"What about a driver's license?"

"I already knew how to drive. I had to take the test, but I got my license with no trouble." He smiled, seeming quite proud of himself. He fished through his pants pocket and pulled out a wallet, and from the wallet extracted a driver's license with perhaps the worst photograph Janna had ever seen. Puck looked like someone had thumped him on the head with a bat, then waited for his eyes to cross and his mouth to gape open before snapping the shot. She sighed and handed it back to him. "You take lousy pictures."

She walked back into her apartment and he followed her in.

"I was talking when the woman took that," he said. "It didn't turn out very well."

"I noticed." She sat on the couch and pointed to one of the armchairs. "Have a seat."

"Something's bothering you," he said.

"Sharp of you to notice. I'm facing some difficult career choices right now. I just got the news back from my agent that I was turned down for a part I really wanted."

"I'm sorry to hear that. And a bit surprised. I can't really imagine anyone having the opportunity to cast you and failing to do so—or perhaps the part was for a homely woman?"

Janna smiled. "Not at all. The part was for a *famous* woman."

"Meaning that you weren't sufficiently well known to be chosen?"

"Precisely." Janna removed the kitten from her shoulder, where it was playing with her hair, and put it on the floor. It looked around for a moment, then scampered off to see what it could discover. She watched it, trying to figure out how best to word what she wanted to say. At last she sighed. "I guess everyone has heard about making deals with the devil."

Puck sat looking at her. He didn't say anything.

"I just want to know if there's any truth to the stories."

"What stories?"

Janna said, "Come *on*. The stories about selling your soul in order to get whatever you want. Signing a contract with the devil—is that possible?"

Puck raised an eyebrow. "If things are that bad, you might just want to consider a new agent."

She glared at him. "I'm not joking. I really want to know."

He said, "I'm trying to put that part of my life behind me . . . but yes. In theory, at least, it's possible. In actual fact, it isn't quite as simple as most people think. First, you have to have a soul that Lucifer particularly wants. And you have to not be headed to Hell already—there isn't much point for him in recruiting you as an officer if you're already going in as enlisted. And of course you have to have some special skill to contribute." Puck leaned back in the armchair and narrowed his eyes. "I sincerely hope you aren't considering it."

"If I were, could you help me?"

"No."

She frowned at him. "No? Just like that? No?"

"I'm doing everything I can to get out of the business."

"Could you at least tell me how to get in touch with someone who can talk to me about this?"

Puck shook his head. "Hell knows now that you're interested. If Lucifer is interested in you, a recruiter will find you."

"Hell knows . . . ?"

"When you speak out loud about selling your soul, Lucifer hears." Puck stood and studied her for a moment, and she thought his eyes looked sad. "I hope you get what you truly want, Janna . . . but if I were you, I'd spend my hours alone contemplating what that was." He headed toward the door. Then he turned to her again.

"Watch the news," he said. "Someone tried to kill your friend Dan today."

Janna walked him to the door and locked it behind him. She checked the time. Almost six. She turned on the television and waited to see if Dan was on it.

Sure enough, he was. A brief interview with him and a short, plump brunette lawyer who was working to get rights for the Hellraised. A couple of well-lit scenes of the parking lot; what was left of Dan's car; Puck doing CPR on a woman; the body of a woman being hauled away in an ambulance; closing shots of WKTU and Dan.

I should have been there, she thought. It would have been a perfect photo op. Those pictures will be on every television screen in the country—and I would have been perfect as the brave-yet-frightened young actress pitching in to save the dying woman, or offering comfort to the bereaved.

She could see herself, face artistically smudged with soot, hair a little mussed, wearing something that was revealing in a sexy, not sleazy, way . . . a shirt with an extra button "accidentally" unbuttoned, or a wide-necked tee with one side of the neck slipped just off her shoulder. She could have been there, too. She's spent the better part of the day with Puck—but when the opportunity for a shot that would hit the cover of *Time* came along, she was home.

She decided that if she got an opportunity to sign a contract with Hell, she'd insist on a clause that would put her in the middle of prime news events.

Chapter 28

Dan leaned back in the seat of Meg's car and tried to forget about the last few hours. Neither he nor Meg had said much since they found out the woman Puck had tried to save had died. Dan had waited around until the police were finally able to talk to him. Then he'd given his statement. The detective he spoke to said the police had plenty of corroborative evidence to support Dan's contention of a letter bomb. He'd mentioned the letters the explosion had scattered across the apartment complex, stating that a lot of them appeared to be hate mail.

Dan still felt strange. Someone had tried to kill him. Someone wanted him dead.

"Meg. Let's stop by Cynthia's house on the way home. I want to visit with my family."

Meg's face looked tight. She'd been in her own world until his voice had interrupted her thoughts, and he could see from the set of her mouth and the look in her eyes that it hadn't been a happy world. She glanced over at him and said, "I'll drop you off, if you don't mind, but I really can't stay to visit. Do you think your sister could drive you home?"

"I'm sure she could." He frowned. "What do you have to do?"

Her lips thinned to a tight line. "Work."

"Related to what happened?"

She glanced over at him. "What makes you say that?"

"You don't get angry often, but you're angry now."

"Someone tried to kill you," she said. "If that someone had been successful with you, I would have died, too. Both of us—the two people who are currently most active in this Great Devil Makeover, and in trying to fix the situation here in North Carolina, would have been dead. And if you don't mind me saying so, I have no wish to be a martyr for the cause."

He nodded. "So what are you going to do?"

"I'm not entirely sure. I have an idea . . . but I don't really want to discuss it until I know if it's even feasible."

She dropped him off, gave him a quick kiss, and waited until Cyn came to the door. But she drove off before he could even double-check to see if his sister would be able to give him a ride home.

The first words out of his sister's mouth were, "You look like shit."

He tried a smile, then gave up the attempt. "You saw the news?"

"Yes."

"I could have lost all of you. Mom . . . you . . . Amy . . . Tom . . . even Arthur . . ."

She hugged him. "I know. I know." He realized she was crying. He hugged her tightly and began to cry, too.

When at last they wiped the tears from their eyes, he said, "Do me a favor, would you? Would you call Mom and Arthur and ask them to come over? I want to see both of them but my car's . . ." He started to giggle, realized it was a delayed reaction to the shock, and even when he realized it, couldn't do anything to make himself stop. "Oh, God. My car. I don't have a flat tire, Cyn. I have a flat car." He stood there laughing while Cynthia stared at him; when the nervous laughter changed to tears, he leaned against the wall and let them flow. "Somebody tried to kill me," he said. "Me. I'm just a damn DJ. I play music and tell a few stupid jokes in the morning to help people wake up. That's all."

Cyn was out in the kitchen, on the phone. Dan realized he was talking to himself.

"That's all I was, anyway. I guess I'm not just a DJ anymore. I'm a celebrity. But if this is what it means to be a celebrity, I don't think I want to be one."

He was calmer by the time Cyn rejoined him in the living room. "Mom and Dad will be here in half an hour. Tom's on his way home, too. He got his supervisor to fill in for him."

Dan leaned against the cool, smooth expanse of wall and closed his eyes. "Thanks," he said.

He heard the soft shuffle of footed jammies on wood floor, followed by a shrill squeal.

"Uncle Danny!"

"Amy," her mother said, "what are you doing up?"

"Uncle *Danny*!" Amy climbed onto the back of the couch before Dan could grab her and shrieked, "Catch me!"

"Jesus!" He caught her in midair. "Don't do that! You almost gave me a heart attack!"

She giggled. "You're funny."

Dan tickled her stomach. She erupted into squeals of laughter as he lifted her over his head and spun the two of them in a circle. He hugged her and fought back the tears. "Hey, Cyn," he yelled, holding Amy upside-down by her ankles. "This belong to anybody?"

Cynthia smiled. The game was an old one, but she didn't mind playing. "Where'd you find it?"

"Outside rummaging in the garbage can."

"Probably a raccoon. Be careful, it might bite."

At the suggestion, Amy bent in half trying to nip Dan's hand. He said, "You don't think it's rabid, do you?"

"Is it foaming at the mouth?"

He grabbed Amy under the arms and held her up. She kicked the air. "Put me down!"

"Yep. What now?"

"Don't they have shots for rabies?"

"NO SHOTS!" Amy yelled.

"Then let's cook it for dinner." He made growling noises and bared his teeth at her, and she screamed again. He put her down and she ran over to the couch and crawled behind it.

He smiled at Cynthia. She smiled back.

When his mother and stepfather arrived, he hugged them both. "Mom . . . Dad," he said, "I'm so glad to see you."

We have so much, he thought. So much, and we take it for granted. We forget how precious family is, and how easy it is to lose.

Chapter 29

Hell's recruiter arrived in a cloud of sulphur and brimstone, with a thunderclap to announce his presence. He stood at the foot of her bed glowing a dull and evil red in the dark room. "I heard you were looking for me," he said.

Janna hadn't been asleep, but she'd been sleepy. Not anymore. Her heart pounded and her mouth dried out. This was an altogether different order of devil than Puck; this monster stood more than eight feet tall—she knew this because her bedroom had an eight-foot ceiling, and the devil had to crouch to stand there. Its wings swept to either side of her bed like curtains, and it leered at her, twisting its nightmare of a face into a grin.

"Ah . . ." she said, staring up at it. "I . . . ah . . ."

"You want to be a resounding success, no matter what the cost. You want to be a brilliant actress, a renowned director, a producer of films both critically acclaimed and commercially successful."

She stared up at it. "Yes."

"You want to be a legend now as well as a legend after you're gone."

She straightened a little. "Yes. That's what I want."

"And you want this success to be guaranteed—you want the guarantee that no matter what you do, you cannot fail."

She had regained her composure. "That's exactly what I want."

"I'm Scumslag. Usually I don't waste my time with recruitment, but we think you have the potential to do a great deal for our organization. We think you are, in fact, potentially one of the most extraordinary candidates we've ever had the pleasure to recruit. So in spite of the fact that I'm in charge of the whole Earthside operation, I've decided to talk with you personally. I've come to discuss terms with you."

Janna smiled. She'd expected when she talked to that spineless excuse for a devil, Puck, that Hell would be interested in her. She felt gratified to discover that Hell shared the high opinion she held of herself. She got out of bed and said, "Yes. Let's discuss terms."

She started out to the kitchen, wearing only the lacy negligee in which she'd gone to bed—she didn't see a need for a housecoat. She'd appeared topless on screen in *Raging Moon*, and doubted that the devil would take much interest in her physical body in any case. Scumslag vanished from behind her and reappeared in front of her, considerably smaller but still frightening in appearance. He had, however, ditched his wings for an elegant black silk suit, a tailored European-cut shirt, and black patent leather wingtipped shoes. His red silk tie had an understated flame pattern woven into the cloth, and his slim leather briefcase looked both expensive and tasteful.

Once again Janna was pleased. Nice to know Hell went first class.

The devil pulled out a chair for her at the kitchen table, then took one for himself. "I'll hit the high points," he said, smiling, "and if you have any questions, just stop me and ask. Since you expressed interest in Satco, I don't feel it's necessary to give you the full recruitment pitch, but . . ." He shrugged and his smile grew broader. She was, for a moment, fascinated by his teeth, which were all tremendously long and pointed. Her first acting job had been as an extra in a horror flick, and she'd had a mouth full of teeth rather like those. She wondered if the devil's were more comfortable than the ones she'd worn.

He pulled out a contract, and she got a good look at his hands. The black, needle-sharp talons were as long as his fingers, and wickedly curved. He was hairless, with batlike ears, curling horns, and eyes as flat and deadly as those of a rattlesnake—pale gold, with square pupils. Those eyes were the only thing he shared in common with Puck, her only other close encounter with deviltry. She imagined that Scumslag would despise Puck for willingly giving up the power and fear that being a devil would confer.

"As far as your Hell-terms," Scumslag said, "we're offering an initial seven-year postmortem hitch. You'll go in as a Demon First Class. If you've made Devil Junior Grade or better by the end of the seven years, you'll be allowed to re-up. Or, of course, you can repent, but I'll be honest with you. Hell has excellent terms of advancement, whereas in Heaven, you stay where you are."

Janna nodded. "So if I fail to make grade, I'll end up in Heaven."

Scumslag raised an eyebrow. "You'll end up in Heaven if you repent. If you fail to make grade, you'll end up as a damnedsoul, and you'll have to work your way up through the ranks from imp. But if you were that sort of a slacker, we wouldn't be interested in you in the first place."

"I see."

"We expect big things from you, Janna, both here

and below. If you decide to take our offer, you'll get a signing bonus, and start off with a salary commensurate with your rank as a human operative, brevetted Demon First Class. That salary, paid to you annually on the first day of the new year, will be in addition to any money you make on your own."

"How much?"

"Seven hundred fifty thousand dollars."

"That's not so much."

"No. It isn't. But if you manage to earn promotions while you're a human agent, you'll get increases in your pay. And of course that doesn't take into account the fact that we're guaranteeing you enormous career success."

Right. She'd forgotten that. She wasn't looking at a salary. She was looking at gravy on top of the millions she'd make as an actress, director, and producer.

"Fine," she said.

She took the contract and looked it over. She would be a major big-budget motion picture star. Hell guaranteed her top billing or equal billing on every project she starred in, and guaranteed, too, that when she chose to move behind the camera, she would continue to have the golden touch. Her entire life would be remarkable; the body of her work would endure in popularity long after her death; she would be a legend.

In return, Hell claimed her soul.

"So how do I go about earning promotions and raises?"

Scumslag smiled. "I can't tell you that."

"Excuse me?"

"I literally can't tell you that. God has prohibited us from saying or doing certain things while we're on Earth, and if I were to tell you what you had to do to earn promotions, I would be breaking that rule."

"So break it."

Scumslag laughed. "You have the right attitude for Hell. Unfortunately for me, I am physically incapable of doing what you ask me. But I've included a copy of God's orders to the Hellraised. If you look at those and see the things we can't do, you'll figure out quickly enough what you'll need to do to earn your wings."

Janna smiled. "I'll be brilliant, hmmm?"

"Brilliant."

"Give me a pen."

Scumslag handed her a beautiful, heavy, enameled fountain pen. "Just sign on the bottom."

As Janna wrote her name, a pin in the side of the pen popped out and stabbed her in the finger. Blood poured across the contract.

"Just write through it," the devil said.

Janna kept on writing.

Chapter 30

Honorial said, "I really thought she'd change her mind. She was willing to work hard. She didn't mind the hours, the sacrifices she had to make to do what she loved. Why did she sign?"

God shook his head. "She wanted a guarantee."

"But Hell can't give her anything she couldn't have given herself."

"No. It can't."

"So she would have been this brilliant actress, this genius director and great producer, all on her own?"

God just looked at him. "What do you think?"

Chapter 31

SATURDAY, JUNE 11TH

Five A.M. came early, especially since sleep had come so late, and since usually he would have had Saturday off. Most of him hoped that Carol, the regular weekend morning jock, would enjoy her vacation, but a small selfish part of him prayed that she'd been harassed by insects to the point where she decided to come home. Nothing would have made that part of him happier than walking into the studio and finding her already in the chair. Dan stopped to wake up Puck on his way out to remind him that he had spots to tape later in the day; then he drove the car he borrowed from the station to work on autopilot.

Sandy hugged him when he went into the studio. "I tried to reach you late last night, but either you weren't home or you just weren't picking up. Your answering machine wasn't working."

"My whole phone wasn't working. People said it rang when they called, but it was dead on my end. The explosion did something to the wiring—the phone company is supposed to have it working again today."

"Oh. Mostly I wanted to let you know I was glad you weren't dead."

"I was pretty glad of that myself."

"The phones here have been going wild. People all over the United States have seen that video clip of Puck doing CPR and trying to save the woman. According to them, he's the greatest thing in redemption since Christ," she said.

"I can imagine. It's such a pity she didn't make it."

Sandy nodded. "Yeah. We could have had her in here, talking about how her life was saved by a devil who'd been reformed by the Great Devil Makeover—" Sandy faltered. "What? Why are you looking at me that way?"

"I just meant," Dan said, "that it was a pity she didn't live. I wasn't thinking of the publicity angle of her being saved by Puck."

"Oh. Yes. I see what you mean."

Dan got ready to take over for her. As she was getting the backpack she frequently carried instead of a purse, he turned back to her and said, "People are getting a little carried away by what a good thing we're all doing, and forgetting why we're doing it."

Sandy nodded. "In light of that, maybe I shouldn't mention the ratings."

"Ratings?"

"They came out yesterday. I can understand why you hadn't heard. Anyway, guess how we did."

"Don't tell me we got nudged by WZZV again."

"We doubled our share."

"What?" Dan looked up from his console and grinned at her. "You're not kidding, are you? And if you are, lie to me."

"I would, but I'm not. We grabbed share from every single station in this town. Even the country and urban stations."

"Yeeeessssss!" Dan leaned as far back in the chair as he could and closed his eyes.

"So it's all right to get a little carried away?"

He laughed. "Yeah. And probably all right to be a little self-congratulatory. I mean, we are doing something good."

"You bet your ass. Bernie's having T-shirts done up with little red devils on them. Sales has been on the phone ever since the ratings from Arbitron came out. All our old accounts are back, and paying more. And we have new accounts all over the place."

"It's turning, isn't it?"

Sandy tipped her head and studied him. "Turning?"

"The state. The economy. It's starting to turn around."

Sandy shrugged. "Too soon to tell. The station is, at least. But I'll bet somebody checking the numbers of people moving out of state would see a drop in *that* statistic."

Dan closed his eyes. Sandy's song was wrapping up. He had two minutes of advertisements to run before he did his opening sequence for the Gunga Dan morning show. "It's going to work, though, Sandy. I can feel it." He pulled his script in front of him and told her, "I believe."

Chapter 32

By the end of his shift he'd interviewed two Raleigh women and the gargoyle they'd adopted, had taken calls from the listeners he was starting to classify as the good, the bad, and the nuts, and had discussed Puck and Puck's progress in between playing the best rock of the '70s, '80s and '90s. When he left the booth he felt *sure* North Carolina was moving toward its own redemption.

But not all at the same pace.

He got two more calls from people who said they were going to get him, and several from people who said they were very sorry to see on television that the car bomb had blown up the wrong person. While the hate calls weren't fifty percent of the calls he was getting anymore, as they had been the first day or two, they still made up about a third of the phone calls that he took over the air, and about a fourth of the ones the station received.

Steve's replacement, a guy named Keene, came in for his first afternoon and Dan had a few minutes to talk to him before he joined Sandy and Darlene for a couple of quick, celebratory drinks over the ratings. The guy seemed nice enough. He was a funny, easygoing redhead the size of a bull moose, and he was congratulatory about the Great Devil Makeover. "I came in to apply for this job because of you," he said. "You're the kind of person this state needs. You know I *stayed* here because of you? I had almost finished packing . . ." He gave Dan a bemused smile. "That would have been a damned shame, too. I love it here."

Dan nodded. "I know what you mean."

The celebration took place at a bar within walking distance of his apartment, a new tavern called The Green Lantern that was next to Darryl's on Old Wake Forest Road. The place had attracted a neighborhood clientele; the college crowd mixed liberally with businessmen stopping in after hours and couples on their way to and from other places. Dan visited at irregular intervals, usually when he was missing Francie. Since the hellish heat of the last few days had finally broken, he dropped the station's car off in the parking lot, changed into Bermuda shorts and his favorite Hawaiian shirt and a pair of athletic sandals, and hiked. That way, he figured, if he and Sandy and Darlene decided to get shit-faced, he wouldn't have to worry about getting the car home. He'd considered calling either Meg or Janna to see if one or the other wanted to join him, but he realized he didn't particularly want to share The Green Lantern.

The crowd was typical of Saturday night; he was there alone, but Sandy brought Julie and Darlene brought her fiancé, whose name Dan thought was Mitch or Rich. He and Sandy and Mitch/Rich kept drinking after Julie and Darlene switched to Diet Cokes. They had a good time, but he had the Sunday morning show, too, and another five A.M. wake-up—and he felt the alcohol, which meant he'd probably gone past enough and into the realm of too much.

He raised the remains of his boilermaker and said, "Final toast for me, folks. To second chances."

The others raised their glasses, he swallowed the last

of his drink, then rose to leave. He felt a little unsteady.

"You want a ride?" Mitch/Rich asked.

"The walk will straighten me out a little," Dan said. He took a deep breath, pulled his shoulders back, wondered if he was overcompensating, then carefully left the bar.

He felt better as soon as he stepped out the door. The night air was cool and summer-scented—he recognized the heavy sweetness of gardenias and the lighter scent of night-blooming jasmine planted along the back of the bar's parking lot. One of those funky things that surprised women—that he knew some flowers by their smells. That was because of Francie, of course. She'd loved flowers.

He started feeling sorry for himself again, and though he knew the alcohol was talking, he let himself listen. He didn't even notice for a moment that a tall, gorgeous woman had joined him and was walking beside him, until she said, "Want a date?"

He jumped and turned to look at her. "No thanks."

"You sure?"

Dan gave her a more thorough assessment. His first impression had been "gorgeous." His second was "most beautiful woman I have ever seen in my life." Her eyes were large and luminous, her lips full, her jaw firm and just square enough. Her hair flowed down to the middle of her bare back in a dark sensuous wave. Her tight sheath dress barely reached to midthigh. She balanced like a dancer on five-inch spiked pumps. She was, he thought, an order above the usual cut of streetwalkers. She was young enough, beautiful enough that she should, at least, have been a high-priced call girl operating out of an expensive apartment. The clothes said streetwalker, though. She was wasting all that beauty on sleaze.

"You aren't my type," he said.

She shrugged and smiled at him. "Your loss," she said. "But if you've never had a succubus, honey, you don't know what you're missing."

He stopped and stared at her. "You're one of the Hellraised?"

"Guaranteed disease-free—you don't even need a rubber with me, sweetheart. And you wouldn't believe what I can do with my tongue."

He shook his head. "You're going to have to do it with someone else."

She rested a hand on his shoulder, and after just an instant, said, "I can be anything you want."

Her voice had changed. Dan turned to chase her away, and found himself face to face with Francie. Not the real Francie—he knew that. This woman was too tall, too voluptuous, and dressed in a way Francie would never have dressed. But the face was Francie's face. The eyes were her eyes. The smile was her smile. Dan felt a lump growing in his throat, felt tears beginning to burn in his eyes.

"Get away from me," he snarled.

Her face melted into the face it had been before. She shook her head and smiled a pitying smile at him. "Like I said, darlin'—your loss." She sauntered back the way she'd come, her hips swinging to a sultry jazz beat that only she could hear. He found himself watching her leave.

She would have been Francie for me, he thought. But she could never have *been* Francie.

He turned at last and trudged down the street toward home.

A few minutes later, cutting through the alley that led to the apartment complex, he heard footsteps. He looked over his shoulder.

Three of the Hellraised were back there. He could

make out the horns on one, the dragging tail of the second, the long claws and pitchfork of the third.

Funny, though—he'd never seen one of the Hellraised carry a pitchfork. He'd decided, after watching interviews and meeting a few and passing them on streets, the pitchfork was just some cliché designed by artists who thought the Devil farmed.

But no. Evidently not.

The trio behind him started walking faster. Dan felt a little uneasy—he knew the Hellraised couldn't hurt him. But his gut didn't know that. He instinctively picked up his own pace a little, trying to make his strides longer but not faster, so they wouldn't know they were scaring him.

Well, they'd know, of course. They were the Hellraised. He tried to remember if he'd read anything about gangs of Hellspawn stalking people through alleys in order to scare them. He couldn't recall any incidents of that sort, but . . .

Their footfalls rang faster. He wished the alley wasn't so long, or that the next break in the brick buildings was closer. He kept wondering why they were following him.

Suddenly he heard them start to run.

Oh, shit, he thought. He bolted. They can't hurt me . . . they can't hurt me . . . he told himself over and over, while he pounded through the alley. They can't do anything to me at all.

But what if they could?

"Faster!" one of them yelled. "Before he hits the street."

He could see the street lights ahead of him. Beyond the alley he could hear the movement of traffic. But in the tunnel of darkness through which he ran, it seemed that only he and his pursuers existed. Adrenaline banished his drunkenness—his terror lent him speed.

"Kill him now," a different voice shouted.

He pumped his arms, picked up his feet, wished he had a job that got him off his ass more often. He was out of shape, and he could feel it almost immediately. Breathe, he thought. Breathe.

Something ripped into his side, threw him off his stride, flung him up against the brick wall while red screaming tearing pain burned through his ribs through his flesh and the night-black world flashed blood-red and pain-white.

Rough hands grabbed him and threw him against the wall again—his head bounced off brick and the night lit up with thousands of white pinprick stars that swirled inches from his face. He fought, kicking and punching; a hand clamped over his mouth and nose and he bit; someone screamed; someone else began punching him in the gut, rhythmically—in, twist, out . . . in, twist, out . . . over and over. He realized the man had a knife. Was stabbing him. He tried to push off the attacker, but the other two men held his hands. The fight went out of him. He sagged. This is it, he thought. I'm dead.

Twin beams of white light shot down the alley, illuminating the three attackers. A car coming. Too late.

Dan saw that his attackers were human, dressed in devil costumes. Their heads came up from what they were doing, they stared for just an instant at the oncoming car.

"Take him with us?"

"Leave him. No way he's going to make it."

"Run!"

Then they ran, leaving the knife still in his gut. He watched them flee. Saw the lines of costumes in the bleaching beam of the mercury headlights—zippers down backs, seams in legs and arms, a tear in one costume that showed a bit of blue denim underneath. Funny to notice such things when he was dying. Dying didn't hurt as much as he'd thought it would, either.

And he thought, Francie, it won't be long now.

The car stopped in front of him, bathing him in its headlights. Someone got out, slammed the door—he heard running feet, this time coming toward him. Then Puck was kneeling over him, staring at the damage, muttering, "No, you can't die, you can't die," and his words got further and further away, as if Dan were falling down a well.

Too late, he thought. I'm doing it anyway.

That seemed almost funny.

Funny.

Which described the way he felt. Warm and cold, and light.

As if he were floating. He looked around him, looked down, and realized he *was* floating. His body lay below him, and he reached for it, but couldn't hold on to himself. Couldn't get back. For a moment he hung there, staring down, watching Puck sending the imp running for help. Funny. He looked so stupid in his bloody Hawaiian shirt and his shorts, with his eyes open and staring. He couldn't even find it in himself to feel much regret. Francie was somewhere ahead of him, not behind him. He looked up. He could feel her presence. Francie.

The devil did something that didn't make sense to him. Soft golden light began pouring from his fingertips and from his eyes, as if for a moment they'd become headlights, too. Dan's gentle, gradual drift away from his body stopped. In fact, it seemed that he was getting closer to himself again.

No, he thought. Francie! I want to go to Francie!

Then he felt himself breathing, and heard again the noise of his heart beating and his blood rushing through his arteries and he felt tremendous pain in his head and chest and stomach, and he heard people running toward him, shouting.

Puck's eyes still glowed. His hands still glowed. The pain lessened.

People he didn't know stood around him, staring down at him.

One of them whispered, "It's a miracle."

Puck said, "Can you hear me, Dan?"

Of course I can, he thought. Don't be ridiculous. But when he tried to speak, he realized his mouth and vocal cords wouldn't respond. Couldn't.

"Dan. Come back." Puck's voice sounded almost angry.

Then he heard Janna's voice, saying, "Dan, sweetheart, you have to pull through this for me. Come on, Dan."

How had Janna found him? How had she known that he needed help? He didn't know, but she'd come. She was with him.

He thought, I am back. I'm back. I'm going to live.

Then the pain got worse one more time—became almost unbearable, as if he were running through a white-hot fire, as if it were burning his lungs and chest and belly to charcoal.

And he screamed.

Chapter 33

Janna made sure she told all the reporters that Dan was her boyfriend. She made sure they knew she was the one who'd knelt beside him in that dark alley and cradled his bloody head on her lap. She expected the early morning news all across the country would have that picture of her, blood-drenched and angry, standing by her man in spite of the danger to her own life.

Scumslag had come to get her—just like in the contract. Got her onsite on time for one hell of a photo op.

The photos would cover the front pages. They also ought to get rid of that female lawyer who'd been hanging around him. If she realized Janna had claimed Dan, she would also realize that she couldn't compete.

She hadn't even panicked when Scumslag materialized in her bedroom again, and when he told her to get dressed and drive to that bar, she hadn't wasted a second in responding. Never let it be said that I can't make the best of an opportunity. Scumslag said her "rescue" of Dan was the first step in her rise to fame and fortune.

She hadn't enjoyed getting bloody, and as soon as Dan turned all clingy and grateful she was ready to get rid of him, but she acted her part perfectly. The loving woman willing to do anything to protect her man.

Dan certainly believed.

Chapter 34

SUNDAY, JUNE 12TH

After the second attempt on his life, Dan found himself with a day off. Sandy stayed over and covered for him and the weekend afternoon DJ was going to come in early. After Dan called Bernie to tell him what had happened, Bernie decided that having Dan away from the station might be good for the station, no matter what he was doing for the ratings.

"If the wackos decide to blow us up," Bernie'd said, "the fact that we were number one when they did it is going to be small consolation."

So Dan woke at seven, hungover, hurting, and with the tune of the song "Mandy" running through his head. He eased out of his waterbed, grateful that Puck and Fetch had done such a miraculous job of fixing it. Puck's miracle with him had been less pain-free. He would have the scars from the knife for the rest of his life. Forty-seven of them. And even though Puck had healed the lethal wounds, he hadn't managed to take away the bruises or a lot of the pain; Dan's entire chest and gut felt like one big bruise. Hurting the way he was, he didn't know that he could have slept at all on a regular bed. Or the couch. Or the floor. Thank Puck for the waterbed.

He limped to the shower, wondering how people who broke their ribs managed to breathe. His chest was on fire and he wanted to hunch over and creep along an inch at a time, and all he had was bruised cartilage. In the shower, surrounded by the steam and enjoying the hot water pounding on his back, he began to feel better. A lot better.

When he caught himself singing a Donny and Marie Osmond song about being "a little bit country and a little bit rock and roll," though, he turned the hot water off entirely and stood in the icy cold spray until he came to his senses. He didn't think he could stand to feel that good.

"What next?" he muttered. " 'Stairway to Heaven'? Something by Tiffany? 'Just When I Needed You Most'? Or maybe a song by Boyz II Men, the Osmonds of the nineties?" He'd never been an aficionado of insipid pop. Not ever. So where was this regurgitation of the sappiest music of all time coming from?

Then he heard them. Out in the living room.

The Bee Gees.

"Aw, *come on*!" He threw on his bathrobe and limped out of his bedroom.

Puck sat on the couch, eyes closed, a blissful expression on his face, listening while the castrati disco gods of the seventies squeaked and squealed.

"Puck?"

"Mmmmm?" The devil didn't open his eyes.

"What are you doing?"

Puck pointed to the stack of vinyl on the turntable. "Listening to my music."

"There's such a thing as going too far," Dan said. He turned the volume down on the stereo. "You can listen to good music. You don't have to develop a taste for this . . . dreck."

Puck sat up. "Excuse me, but *this* is what I *like*. This is what I've liked for a long time. This is *my* music."

"This is what you listened to in Hell?" Actually, Dan could see that. He guessed even music got what it deserved.

"What *I* listened to. Not what everybody listened to. *I* wasn't going to listen to elevator music."

"Elevator music?"

"Yeah. Ozzy Osborne, Black Sabbath . . . like that." He got a smug look on his face. "I listened to counterculture," he said, and Dan was almost certain he could hear a note of pride in the devil's voice.

Chapter 35

Meg stepped into the restaurant, glanced over her shoulder just to be sure she hadn't been followed, and said, "I'm meeting someone," to the maitre d'.

"Certainly, madam. Would you care to wait at the bar until your party arrives?"

"If you don't mind, I'll just wait here."

He smiled at her and said, "You'll find comfortable chairs over there, and you'll have no trouble seeing the door."

She nodded, walked into the little waiting room, and took a seat.

She was still angry—she was angry that people had tried to kill Dan, but her anger extended far beyond that. Those killers felt they could make liberal North Carolinians stop supporting equal rights for the Hellraised by eliminating him. Once again religious fanatics and right-wing hate groups wanted to dictate the actions of others, but this time they were going to fail. She was going to turn the whole thing around on them.

She saw Puck drive into the parking lot a few minutes after she did. He came in wearing a pair of dark glasses that hid his eyes—the last sign that he was one of the Hellraised. He spotted her quickly and strolled over. His expensive silk suit, elegantly cut to emphasize his broad shoulders and lean waist, and the professional cut of his hair, which fell boyishly across his brow while still giving an impression of style, went a long way in disguising the fact that he was still quite ugly. If you look rich, Meg thought, ugliness starts looking a lot like good breeding.

"He hasn't arrived yet?"

"Not yet."

"Then we have a little time to discuss this."

"Not much. Stay within earshot, but out of sight. I don't want him to realize you've been in the restaurant the whole time. When I say I've asked a friend to join us, wait five minutes, then come over. I want him prejudiced in your favor when he meets you."

Puck nodded. "I'll just get a magazine and wait until the two of you are seated—then I'll find a convenient place.

"Fine."

Puck moved off, settled into a chair, picked up a magazine, and seemed to disappear. Meg saw him sitting there, but he managed somehow to give the impression that he was a part of the decor, not someone who ought to be noticed. It was a pretty good trick, she thought.

She waited only a few minutes more. Then a good-looking man in his midthirties came through the doors. He was alone, and like Meg, he checked just to be sure he wasn't being followed. Sandy-haired, bearded and muscular, he looked vaguely uncomfortable in the dinner jacket and tie that he wore. Meg could imagine him in hiking boots, khaki shorts and a Save Our Wetlands T-shirt. Probably carrying a picket sign. In fact, she thought she recognized his face from one of the multitude of mailers she'd received from Forever Wilderness.

She sighed. Politics does indeed make strange bedfellows, she thought.

She stood, and he glanced over at her and gave her a tentative smile. "Ms. Lerner?"

She smiled back. "The same."

"Kyle Haversham. I'm president of Forever Wilderness, Inc."

They shook hands, followed the maitre d' to a table, then ordered. They engaged in small talk until the entrees arrived, or rather, Kyle engaged in small talk while Meg basically engaged in small listening. He discussed his success in locating and acquiring a large tract of forested land in Connecticut; the pending legislation that would mandate an annual tax on all firearms—Haversham hoped fervently that it would pass and Meg forced a smile and agreed with him; and the recent criminalization of tobacco use in California.

"That's one law I'd like to see spread everywhere," Haversham said.

Meg nodded. Politics, she thought. Strange bedfellows. She said, "Certainly," and hoped her smile didn't look as forced as it felt. Evidently it didn't, for Haversham kept talking.

"These conservative North Carolinians shout about the right to personal choice, but I don't see where smoking is a right. It's like seat-belt laws—if people can't be trusted to act in their own best interests, then the government needs to step in and act for them."

Meg wondered if she could throw up on Haversham on her way out without blowing her deal. How could he be so blithe about giving the government more power to encroach in the lives of its citizens? But of course he assumed it would only encroach in the ways he wanted.

With the arrival of their meals, though, their conversation took a turn toward business.

"The Vaillaird Bank consortium has been in touch

with you about buying your Pender County holdings," Meg said.

"As far as I know, it's been in touch with every officer of Forever Wilderness. We aren't interested in selling."

Meg nodded. "I know. And I do understand your position. You intend to hold the land as a wild preserve in perpetuity, which I think is noble. And a wonderful cause. I donated to your organization once," she added, feeling like a creep for using such a cheap ploy to curry favor. She intended to do worse, though, if she had to.

"Then you understand that once we buy a piece of property, we must retain it."

"Under most circumstances, yes. In this instance, however, I think you'll find that you further your own cause by selling."

He raised his eyebrows and started to argue, but Meg held up a finger.

"Hear me out. I know where you stand on this. According to the head of the consortium, all of your people were appalled by the archconservative stance of most of the consortium members."

"Do you realize that, collectively, the group that wants to buy that land has invested in almost every capitalist sweatshop operation around the globe?"

Meg said, "I know several of the members of the group fairly well. While I like some of them a great deal as people, I find their politics and moral stances on issues repugnant." *As repugnant as I find yours,* she thought. "However, I think you'll find it interesting to know that the consortium is acting as a middleman for another interested group."

"Really?"

Meg nodded. "And this is strictly confidential, but if you're interested, I'd be willing to disclose the identity of the actual buyer."

"Of course I'm interested. You think this other buyer will change my mind, hmm?"

"Let me put it this way. The final buyer is a hell of a long way from being an archconservative." Meg smiled. "Have you been following the local furor over the Great Devil Makeover?"

"Of course. I think everyone has."

"How do you feel about it?"

"About what?"

Meg had to be careful how she worded this. She wanted the most anticonservative wording she could find; she thought Haversham would respond to that better than he would to the moderate phrasing she herself would have found preferable. She said, "About the general North Carolinian refusal to grant any sort of rights or protections to people who, through no fault of their own, have been forced to live here and are incapable of living anywhere else?"

He looked a little surprised. "To tell you the truth, I hadn't looked at it in quite that way."

Meg hadn't thought so. "No? I'm surprised. I've been looking at it that way for a while, so of course it seems obvious to me." She leaned forward, resting her elbows on either side of her plate, and said, "I do family practice. But I saw this tremendous injustice being done, so I sat down with some colleagues of mine who work for the ACLU. I presented work I'd done toward the initiation of a class action antidiscrimination suit against the state."

Haversham grinned at her. "That's terrific."

"Thanks. But that's a slow, slow process. Meanwhile, discrimination—at least discrimination by conservative and religious elements in the state—prevents the Hellraised from finding gainful employment, buying property, or becoming productive members of society."

"I can see that."

"The Hellraised want to buy this land. They'll use it to employ themselves."

"Damn." Haversham sighed. "Look, under the circumstances, I'd almost consider selling it to them. But you see, they approached us about it before. They want to build an amusement park on the site—and we simply can't permit that. If they wanted to buy the land to maintain as wilderness . . ." He shrugged.

They can't employ themselves running a wilderness, you idiot, she thought. She was going to have to crawl a little lower. "How many conservatives live in Pender County?" Meg asked. "And religious fundamentalists? How many of those?"

"The place is full of them."

Meg nodded and leaned back. "How do they feel about your organization?"

"They hate us."

"Are they tolerant of you?"

"Hell, no. Those polluting money-grubbing cigarette-smoking Jesus-shouting gun nuts fight us every time we turn around."

"How do you think they'd feel about having a Hell-run amusement park in their back yards?"

Haversham laughed. "They'd shit."

"I know."

She smiled at him.

He smiled at her.

She said, "It's a rather petty thought, isn't it?"

"Pretty petty. Yes." He kept smiling.

Meg worked the corner of her cloth napkin into a tube and rolled it forward and back across the table. Forward and back. Forward and back. She looked at the napkin while she said, "They aren't going to be tolerant of their own free will."

"No."

"Not of you. Not of the Hellraised. Not of anyone who's different than them."

"No."

Meg glanced up at him. "I'll paraphrase something you said, if you don't mind. If they won't do what's good for them of their own free will, then someone should make them do it. They won't accept the Hellraised on their own. *Make* them accept."

"I like it." He paused, glanced out the window beside them at the steady flow of traffic, then looked back at her. "I'm curious, though. I can see why you're involved with this—I can tell you're the sort of person who cares. Who is willing to take on causes. Who pays attention to global concerns, and won't just watch the world be swallowed by the money mongers. But I get the feeling there's more to it for you than just the obvious."

"Of course." Meg gave him a candid smile. "Someone sent Dan Cooley a letter bomb the night before last. I was with him when it went off. If I *hadn't* been with him, he would probably be dead now."

"Dan Cooley . . . Dan Cooley . . ." He frowned. "I can't say the name rings a bell."

"Dan Cooley. Also known as Gunga Dan."

His eyes widened slightly. "Gunga Dan the DJ?"

"Yes."

"I heard about the bombing. Well, who hasn't? You know him?"

Meg smiled. "We're good friends."

"I'm impressed." Haversham took a sip of his water and leaned back in his chair. "I'm also inclined to recommend to the rest of the committee that we go with this deal. Before we can even think about it, though, we'll have to have a couple of concessions."

"Such as?"

"We get an equivalent grant of wild land somewhere else in the state."

"That should be quite simple."

"We stay completely out of the public eye. The consortium who bought the land from us will have to take any pressure for selling it."

"I thought of that. That's why the Hellraised were willing to work through a middleman this time. The middleman will serve as your buffer; the consortium doesn't care what anyone thinks of them, as long as they make their profit."

"Isn't that the way?"

Meg nodded. "It is. Anything else?"

Haversham's eyes got a shifty look. "I'd like to meet one of the . . ." His voice dropped. ". . . one of the Hellraised before I take this back to my colleagues."

Meg smiled. "Of course. As luck would have it, I invited Puck to join us. I thought you'd like to meet him. He's running late—he has quite a busy schedule, between public appearances and doing radio promotions—but I'm sure he'll be along soon."

Five minutes later, Puck strolled up to the table, led by the maitre d'. Haversham seemed surprised to find the devil so urbane and charming. Meg, pleased at how well they were getting along, excused herself for a few moments. Puck had asked Meg when she called him to enlist his help if she wouldn't mind letting him talk with whomever the Wilderness Foundation sent, just for a while. When she returned, they were deep in conversation. Puck glanced at her and hung one hand below the table to give her a thumbs-up sign. That sign meant he could take it from there.

"Gentlemen," she said, "I hate to eat and run, but I have some late work to do on a divorce case for tomorrow morning. Kyle," she shook his hand, "the consortium will be in touch with you tomorrow. If you'd like to talk with me again . . ."

"No, no." He smiled, the smile entirely too broad and toothy. "Not at all. We'll be, I think, more than happy to sell the land. I've been discussing details with Puck, and Devil's Point sounds like a wonderful place. No one mentioned to me that they were bringing back extinct species."

She smiled. Good of Puck to think of that angle. It seemed to have been the clincher.

Chapter 36

Down in the darkness, down in the hot black twisting passageways of Hell, where the damned wept and the doubly damned made them weep, Lucifer sat in his palace; the bitter Prince of Hatred gloated at the shifting tides of a silent war that he waged eternally and had waged since the first human wished an enemy into eternal torture and thereby damned himself. The tides, so fickle of late, now shifted strongly in Lucifer's favor.

Above, in the world of light and the living, where all choices still remained and all options were always open, he felt his servants push open a floodgate . . . and as the leading edge came open, his enemies, flailing and protesting, fought its movement and by fighting gave it the anger and the hatred it needed to move the rest of the way.

God grant me a good enemy, he thought, for there are certainly times when an enemy can open doors no friend ever would.

Chapter 37

Janna picked up the phone.

"Janna? It's Kate Matorsi."

"Hello, Kate." Janna wondered if, given her guaranteed oncoming success, she ought to dump her agent.

"I have some wonderful news for you."

"Really?"

"I just got a call from Anton Leighton-White. He was at the reading that you did the other day for *When the Owl Cries*."

"I remember the name—but he wasn't one of the important people there. He was just sitting in."

"That's right. He's another director working for the same producer. He liked your reading, he liked your look, and he was impressed by the note you sent to the producer. Said you were a real professional and a class act."

"That's nice of him."

"Sweetheart, we don't give a shit about nice. He was sitting in to see if any of the people who were wrong for *Owl* were right for his film, which is basically *Jurassic Park* meets *Raiders of the Lost Ark*. He sent me a script for it; it's wonderful, you have the lead if you want it, and the money they are willing to pay you is beyond the dreams of avarice, kiddo. This movie will be next summer's major summer release."

Janna sat there, thunderstruck. This was it. The big break. Already.

"Speechless, huh?" Kate said.

He'd liked her. He'd liked her enough to give her the lead in a major movie. "Wow," she said.

Kate had to go, but said she'd call back shortly.

Janna hung up the phone and lay down on the couch. Major motion picture. With her as the lead.

He'd liked her.

Or had he?

Maybe it was the contract kicking in. Maybe he hadn't liked her until after she'd signed it.

It didn't matter. Major motion picture. Tons of money, summer release, action-adventure heaven.

Maybe he hadn't liked her at all. Maybe she hadn't been good enough to earn the part.

It doesn't matter, she told herself again. This is my big break. This is where I start to fly.

Maybe he hated me. Maybe I have nothing to do with this at all.

She stared at the ceiling, poised on the brink of success, and found that it wasn't as exciting as she'd thought it would be. She wanted to know that he'd really liked her. She wanted to know that he thought she was wonderful. And she couldn't know that, because her contract with Hell could make him give her the part even if he loathed her. She would never know if he'd liked her work; would never again know if anyone really liked her work.

And it mattered.

Chapter 38

MONDAY, JUNE 13TH

Four A.M. and the phone was ringing. Ringing. Dan flopped across the waterbed and picked it up before the answering machine could cut in on him.

Someone mumbled a long string of words at him. The only one that stuck was "FBI."

"FBI?" he murmured. He lay on his back with his eyes closed tightly, willing himself not to wake up completely, because he still had an hour until he had to get up for work.

More mumbling. He gathered that the FBI had, with assistance, picked up three men for questioning. He thanked the caller, hung up the phone, and went immediately back to sleep.

The alarm went off at five. He sat up, for a moment completely disoriented.

"Did someone call me?" he asked the room.

The room certainly knew but didn't answer.

He got up and got ready for work, sure that he'd gotten a phone call in the middle of the night, but completely unable to imagine what it might have been about. He had the nagging feeling that it had been important. He didn't know why.

"I might have dreamed it," he muttered. He had

annoying dreams like that. Dreaming that he was getting up and getting ready for work, driving there, doing the show—then having the alarm go off and finding out that it didn't count, and that he had to do it all again. Or dreaming that he got up to go to the bathroom, was standing in front of the toilet taking a leak, not feeling any better for having done it, and waking up when he couldn't stop to discover that he was mere seconds away from a complete bladder failure. He always felt cheated by those dreams. He thought if he had to go through the annoyance, it ought to count for something.

Five A.M. was too early to call friends and family to see if they'd called him.

He passed Puck on the couch, and Fetch curled in a little ball by the door. Neither moved as he went by. He dropped a candy bar beside the imp—Fetch had been spending time cleaning up the house at night, and he didn't think the little monster ever got a thank you from Puck. He didn't bother to wake them. Even if either of them knew that the phone had rung, they wouldn't have known who called. Puck had his own schedule, anyway, and maintained his own list of obligations, meetings, promotions and autographings. He might have a full day planned. He might need his sleep.

He and Dan shared the house, but even that wouldn't be for much longer. The elegant Deerfield Crossing apartment complex had offered the devil a two-bedroom furnished apartment at the end of the month, rent free, in exchange for his doing major promotional work for them. So Dan only had another half month of waking up in the middle of the night to the serenading of the Partridge Family, the Jackson Five, and Abba.

When he got to work, he still hadn't remembered

who had called, and he was beginning to be fairly certain that he'd dreamed the entire incident; then, however, Sandy gave him two thumbs up through the glass as he walked into the lobby, and when he gave her a puzzled look and a shrug and mouthed the word "What?" she gave him a look of sheer disbelief.

He stepped into the studio, she finished announcing her last set, and closed the mike.

"What do you mean, 'What?' you moron. I thought the fact that they caught them so fast would have had you jumping up and down for joy."

Something clicked into place. "FBI," he said.

"Ri-i-i-i-i-i-ght." Still with the look that said, Dan Cooley, you came to work without your brain again.

"Yeah. I got a phone call in the middle of the night. But I was asleep. I went back to sleep after the call, and . . ." He shrugged. "To be honest with you, Sandy, I didn't remember anything when I woke up except that either the phone had rung or I dreamed that it did."

"Shit. Doesn't the detachable model give you problems sometimes?"

Dan knew she referred to his mind; he didn't bother to ask, nor did he dignify her comment with a response. Instead, he asked, "How did they get them?"

"According to the AP wire story, one of them got caught trying to dump a bunch of letters and another letter bomb in the mail—all of them addressed to you. The box he used for the letter bomb wouldn't fit into the slot, and a police officer who happened to be driving by stopped because he was making such a ruckus, saw what he had, and took him in." Sandy grinned. "He decided if he was going down, he wasn't going to do it alone. He ratted on both the other guys who were in on it with him."

"Three guys. I thought from all the letters, there had to be more than that."

"Evidently not." Sandy passed him the chair. "Incidentally," she said, "expect a lot of ugly phone calls."

Dan said, "Really? Those guys had supporters even after they killed that woman?"

Sandy shook her head vehemently. "Wrong kind of ugly. They've been calling here since the first AP story went out over the news demanding that we lynch the guy."

"You and me?"

Sandy rolled her eyes. "Christ, no. You did leave without your brain this morning. No. The state. North Carolina. They're calling in from all over the country."

"They are?"

"Lines have been swamped all night long. You're everybody's hero."

She was right.

"Gunga Dan, you're on the air."

"Hi. I'm calling from Denver, Colorado," a cheerful man said, "and I just wanted to say that anyone who doesn't think you're doing a great job can go to Hell."

Dan winced. "Thanks for your support—but we still believe in freedom of thought and speech here in North Carolina." <click> "Gunga Dan, go ahead."

"I'm calling from Valdosta, Georgia, your Hell away from home . . ."

"I think you mean your home away from Hell."

"Just proves you never lived here."

" 'You will never find a more wretched hive of scum and villainy . . .' " Dan said, mimicking Alec Guinness's voice and quoting from *Star Wars*.

The caller laughed. "Maybe you *have* lived here. Anyway, I wanted to say that there are worse things in the world than devils in your neighborhood. Religious prejudice, willful ignorance, racism, closed-mindedness and intolerance all come immediately to mind."

"If you'd added halitosis and farting in elevators, you would have listed the seven deadly sins." <click> "Gunga Dan—talk to me."

"I love you, Gunga Dan. I want to have your baby."

"She might object to being carted around by a stranger," he said. <click> "You're on the air. Say something interesting."

"I think we ought to hang those three guys from the tallest tree in the state."

Dan sighed. "Satan is recruiting on the other side of town. If you want to go to Hell, call him." <click> "Gunga Dan . . ."

And so it went. He didn't bother to play music. He announced the call letters as often as he had to, he handed off to Marilyn every hour on the hour so she could do the real news, he mocked the murderous thugs and made them look like idiots on the air, and tried to make the people who weren't out for blood look smart and funny. Subtle reinforcement—vigilantes are bad, reasonable people are good, he said in a thousand jokes and wisecracks and sly digs. Maybe it would matter. Maybe.

When his shift finally ended, he thought he would have to drag himself home a piece at a time, because he was too tired to move his body all at once.

He stepped out into a June oven to find Puck leaning on the station car waiting for him.

"I need your help," Puck said. "Can we talk?"

"Sure." Dan frowned. "But why in the world would you wait out here? It's nice and cool inside . . ." He flushed. "Right. This probably still seems nice and cool to you."

"I have to admit I don't have a lot of sympathy for

you folks who go around all the time complaining about the temperature."

"I guess not." He shrugged and grinned. "However, if you want to talk to me, I'd rather do it in air conditioning."

Puck waved to his car. "I'll drive. Or we can just sit in the parking lot."

"Parking lot's fine."

They got in and Puck started the car and the air conditioner. The two of them sat, waiting.

"So what do you want to talk about?" Dan finally asked. "What kind of help do you need?"

"A favor."

"You saved my life," Dan said. "I certainly think I can do you a favor."

"You're making too much of that," Puck said. "I just did what I had to do."

"I'd have been dead if you hadn't done it. What do you need?"

Puck winced. "It's major."

"How major was saving my life?"

The devil sighed deeply. "Meg and I talked to a representative of Wilderness Forever, Inc., yesterday."

"On a Sunday?"

"It was a secret meeting. No one was supposed to know about it. But we ironed out most of the problems that stand between the Hellraised and that piece of property."

"Good."

"I see a major problem in the future, however."

"Which is?"

The devil turned and studied him. "The people buying the land from the wilderness people and selling it to the Hellraised are . . . um . . ." He chuckled softly. "Let me put it this way. They'd sell their own grandmothers to Lucifer if they could turn a buck on the deal, and many of their previous dealings prove this. When they sell us the land and we try to get our permits to build on it, people are going to know who they are. Their . . . ah . . . mercenary and somewhat callous record will be on public display, and people will equate them with us. We're going to face a lot of resistance unless someone who has gained the respect of the people of North Carolina stands up for us and says he supports the Hellraised. If you say you think the project will be good for the state, people will support it."

Dan nodded. "I can see that. I think the project *will* be good for the state." He smiled. "But, Puck, I *don't* support the Hellraised. I support the right of the Hellraised to seek second chances for themselves and to find redemption. That's a long way from supporting Hell's agenda."

The devil nodded. "Yes, yes . . . I misspoke. I know how you stand on the issues—I just was a bit careless in my wording."

"It happens. But you want me to say that I'm in favor of seeing Devil's Point built? That I think it will be good for the economy, and that it will give the Hellraised employment that isn't directed entirely at temptation?"

"If you would. I honestly think you are the one man in the state who could smooth the way for us to get Devil's Point off the planning table and into production."

Dan rested a hand on Puck's shoulder. "You saved my life. I owe you a favor. And I'll be more than happy to tell people what I think about the project. You aren't asking me to lie, after all."

"No." Puck smiled. "No. I'm not. I wouldn't do that—it would cost me our friendship, and I know it."

Chapter 39

TUESDAY, JUNE 14TH

Tuesday, Meg called Dan after the show. He'd talked to her only once since the story of how Puck had saved his life had come out. She'd been somewhere between cool and frosty—after letting him know she was glad he wasn't dead, she didn't have much else to say.

He couldn't really blame her. She hadn't known he was dating Janna at the same time that he was dating her. She apparently thought he hadn't been seeing anyone else—and evidently was offended that he hadn't been exclusively hers. Now she sounded crisply professional. "Puck said you were willing to act as spokesman for the Devil's Point project. We're ready to go on the sale of the land. Can you meet with everyone at my office?"

He leaned back on his couch and closed his eyes. The day had been as tough as Monday. Someone had leaked the story that the three Devil Bombers had started building five other bombs, and notes and journals targeting others sympathetic to the Hellraised had supposedly been found at the scene. Call-ins had been heavy and draining. "What time?"

"Three."

Dan looked at his watch—already two. He'd have to shower, shave again, change clothes . . .

He sighed heavily, hoping she'd get the hint. She didn't. Instead, she said, "It's important, Dan. Really important—to Puck and to a lot of other Hellraised souls who won't find a good second chance elsewhere."

"I can be there." He rolled his eyes at Fetch, who sat in the corner of the living room sucking on one of his toes. Fetch grinned at him. Dan grinned back.

The meeting turned out to be as awful as he'd dreaded. By five o'clock the environmentalists were calling the old-money contingent crazed imperialistic capitalists and planet killers. By six, the old money was calling the environmentalists tree-hugging fascists and eco-Nazis. The Hellraised contingent sat in the middle of the melee grinning over their future clients from both camps.

By seven, Dan had a headache that would have killed a blue whale. Or a blue chip stock. To keep one shoe of his hyperbole firmly planted in each camp.

He listened and listened, and no one got anywhere near middle ground. The temperature in the room hit 90, with tempers fifteen or twenty degrees hotter than that. Finally, Dan slammed his fist on the table and said, "Hey assholes! Listen to me! Sell the Hellspawn the land—which is all we came to do—and let's get out of here. None of you people are going to convince anyone else that you're right. None of you will shut your mouths long enough to listen to what anyone else has to say. And you don't want to listen anyway. You just want everyone else to listen to you." He stood up, his voice getting louder. "Well, I'll tell you something that might surprise you. Nobody wants to hear what you have to say, either. You're ALL full of shit, and you're ALL assholes!"

Meg glared at him, and he realized that somewhere along the way, he'd crossed the line between acceptable and unacceptable behavior, at least in her eyes. She said, "I was handling the meeting."

The chip on her shoulder plus four hours of listening to idiots got the better of him. Before he could stop himself, he blurted out, "No you weren't. You were trying to build a consensus between people with no common ground. We don't *need* a consensus. All we need is for these people to sell their land, for those people to buy it, and for *them* to turn around and sell it to the Hellraised. That's all. It's so simple. And either the econuts came to sell their land or they didn't. And if they didn't, they should just shut the fuck up and go home. And either the imperialist assholes came to buy it or they didn't. That's all anybody needs to know."

One of the consortium members said, "This is the man who's going to make our selling land to the Hellraised acceptable?"

"No," Meg said, her voice cool. "I don't think he is."

Dan's eyes narrowed. "Well, just so there won't be any doubt, *sweetheart*, I'll guarantee you that I'm not. You want somebody to sell your project, it can be somebody else."

He started to leave. Puck rose from the far end of the table. "Dan," he said.

Dan's gut knotted. He turned slowly and looked at the devil. "Puck, I owe you for saving my life. If you insist that this is want you want me to do to repay you, then I will." He stared at the roomful of angry faces glaring up at him. "But I don't *want* to help anymore. You—yes. But not these people." He put his hand on the doorknob and twisted. "If you decide you still want me to tell people I'm in favor of the project, you can tell me about it tonight."

The whole drive home, he stewed. But by the time he'd changed into a pair of shorts and his purple, orange, and green macaw shirt, dropped back into his easy chair, and put his feet up, he realized he'd been wrong. Big-time wrong. He'd been incredibly rude to Meg, and Meg hadn't done anything to deserve it. He'd been rude to a group of people who had neither needed nor wanted his opinion of them.

I was tired, he told himself. *I've been dealing with people as ignorant and frustrating as those were all day long. Well, all week long.*

He closed his eyes.

Actually, shithead, he told himself, *that's what you do for a living. If you can't cut it anymore without blowing up at a friend or the people your friend is working with, maybe you should look into a different job. One that keeps you away from people.*

Things were already bad enough between Meg and him. The second he saw the news with Janna—obviously in love with him—giving a statement to the press, he knew that Meg was going to be angry. Hurt. She was going to feel cheated and lied to.

And now he'd humiliated her in front of the people whose deal she was trying to broker by acting like an asshole. He'd said a lot of things that he might have meant, but that he didn't have any real right to say. Not then, anyway. Not there. No one was paying to hear his opinions at that moment.

He groaned. "Fetch," he said, "I said some truly rotten things to Meg. You think she'll forgive me?"

Fetch looked at him and slowly shook his head.

"Thanks for the reassurance, dude." He scratched the back of the imp's head, and it began to make a sort of rumbling, purring noise. With the other hand, he picked up the phone and dialed Meg's number. He got her machine. "Meg, if you're there, pick up. I need to grovel."

She didn't answer.

He called her office, and got the machine there, too.

"Meg, I'm sorry I was such a jerk. I could give you a lot of reasons, but none of them would make the situation any better. Please forgive me."

He waited twenty minutes, hoping that she'd been en route to her uncle's place from work, and tried her machine again. This time Ed picked up.

"Ed. It's Dan."

"I recognized the voice on the machine the first time. You made quite an ass of yourself at the meeting."

"I know. May I talk to Meg? I need to beg forgiveness."

"She isn't home yet. But I wouldn't worry about it too much. Your outburst was like a bucket of ice water dumped on the participants. They shut up after you left and got to work. I'll thank you here and now—if you hadn't blown up like that, we'd probably still be there."

"That was what I was afraid of," Dan admitted. "And I had a long, shitty day."

"Well, the land was sold, then sold again, all the documents were signed, sealed, and copied, inordinate amounts of money changed hands—including enough that went directly to Meggie that she'll be able to buy that house she's been wanting. I should be able to get my guest bedroom back now."

Dan breathed a relieved sigh. "You don't know how pleased I am to hear that."

"Why? Did you have designs on my guest bedroom?"

Dan laughed again.

Ed laughed with him. "Don't be too relieved, though. I think Megan is still royally pissed at you."

"She has every right to be. Please have her call me when she gets there. Tell her I'm—"

His doorbell rang. "Could you hang on for just a second?"

"Of course."

He ran to his door. To his surprise, Meg stood at the door. "Meg!"

"I can't stay—"

"I'm so sorry—"

"—and I didn't stop by to hear you beg forgiveness. As far as I'm concerned, we don't have a personal relationship, so your behavior affected no one but you. The people who were there got to see the real Dan Cooley, and they weren't impressed, but that's your problem, not mine."

She didn't look angry. She just looked cold. Professional. He realized he wanted to see her radiant smile and hear her loony laugh, and at the same instant he realized that he probably never would again. That had been reserved for the private Dan Cooley, not the public one.

Meg continued. "Puck still wants you to represent the Devil's Point project, and so do the rest of the Hellraised who were present at the meeting. They've put together a standard 'spokesman' contract, I've vetted it to make sure there aren't any elements that shouldn't be in there—"

"Like selling my soul."

"—like selling your soul—though if I were you, I wouldn't worry. They'll probably get it at bargain prices a few years down the road. If you don't mind, I'd like for you to sign it. I need to get back—I'm not through with the final portion of the meeting yet."

"Can I look it over for a couple of days?"

Her eyes went even colder, and got that distant look in them again, and she said, "Don't you trust me?"

The woman who had dedicated her life to doing good law for the financially disadvantaged accusing him of not trusting her—that hurt. "Yes, I do," he said. "I can't think of anyone in the world I trust more than you. But I don't want to sign a contract that might in some way conflict with previous obligations. I *have* previous obligations through my work with the radio station, and you don't know what they are or how they might conflict."

She nodded. "Then certainly, look it over tonight. The Devil's Point development team has a press conference scheduled for tomorrow, though, to announce the sale of the land and the planned number of outside jobs the Devil's Point contract will create. I'd like to know you are in our camp by the time we meet the press tomorrow."

"Our camp . . ." he said to her retreating back.

He closed the door slowly, and went back to his chair, and sat down, frowning. Then he realized the phone was still off the hook. He picked it up. "Ed? You still there?"

"Yes."

"Sorry about that. Meg was just here."

"Oh. Then I guess everything's okay again."

Dan thought about that for a second. "No. I don't think it is."

Chapter 40

Meg said, "He wants to look the contract over, of course. I did let him know you were eager to get his signature on it before the press conference tomorrow."

Puck turned to the other Hellraised who sat around the table. "That will be fine," he said. "We know we want him to represent us. He's a good man, and if he needs a little time, we're willing to wait."

The other Hellraised—a dark angel named Canthoniel; another devil, this one named Roiling Pusbucket; and an absolutely gorgeous incubus whose name Meg couldn't remember because he kept smiling at her—nodded their agreement.

"Then if we don't have anything else—" she started to say, but Puck stopped her.

"We've been discussing the matter," Puck said. "While you were gone, I mean. We're going to need a human lawyer to represent the Devil's Point project, and those of us who work on it. Hell's lawyers would certainly be willing to consult, but they haven't taken the bar in North Carolina so they can't practice here." He paused. "Well, some of them passed the bar in North Carolina, but I don't think the state allows lawyers to practice after they're dead."

"I think the state might have a problem with that," Meg agreed. "I know a few business and corporate lawyers who would be able to take you on as clients," Meg said. "Though they might not want to . . ."

"Exactly." Puck smiled at her. "And honestly, we don't want any lawyer. We need a good, honest, upstanding person. An idealist. Someone compassionate, someone who sees beyond our exteriors to the people we once were . . . and could be again."

"I'm not a corporate lawyer, and you're going to be a corporation. I do family practice."

Puck nodded. The other Hellraised nodded. "We all know you're doing good work. Admirable work. We realize that you've spent a great deal of time and effort creating a practice that permits people in lower income brackets to find good representation." Puck smiled.

Meg waited, listening.

"Your idealism extended to helping another disadvantaged section of the North Carolina population: us." Puck tapped his chest, and his expression grew serious. "I'm the first fruits of your work, Meg. I'm the start. You can do more, though; you can reach more of us."

"What about my family practice?"

"Keep it. We won't have much work for you for a while."

"But when you do, your work will eat up my time."

Puck shrugged. "Then you hire partners. Secretaries, legal assistants, interns. By then, your work with us will subsidize your family practice. You'll be able to do *pro bono* work, expand your activism, make the changes in the system that you want to make."

He handed her a folded piece of paper. She unfolded it. "This is a check for half a million dollars," she said.

"It's a retainer. Against this year's expenses. If we go over that in work, bill us. And we can afford another check like that to begin the new year, and in six-month increments thereafter."

"A million dollars a year."

"To start with. If we're as successful as we hope to be, you'll make much more."

She looked at them. She looked at the check. She looked back at them, and frowned. "What are the strings, Puck? Contract on my soul? Retirement at sixty-five, damnation in ten more?"

Puck flushed and looked down at his hands. When he looked at her again, she could see the pain in his eyes. "Even you," he said sadly. "When I try to do something good, something right, even you see an ulterior motive."

She looked down at the check again, feeling her cheeks grow hot. "Damn. I'm sorry, Puck." She looked up at him. "I know you need a good lawyer. And I know I could do a good job for you. Can. I *can* do a good job for you. It just isn't the career I planned, you know?"

He nodded. "Life is what happens while you're making other plans."

She smiled. "So I've heard. So what will I do for this million dollars a year?"

Puck said, "We want to see Devil's Point succeed, of course, so first you'll probably be dealing with the people who are out to put roadblocks in our way. Once the project is off the ground, we'll move to broader concerns. We want representation in local government. We want full citizenship, the right to vote. We'll pay taxes, but we want to get something for our tax dollars. We want to be mainstreamed into society. We want you to give us a shot at taking advantage of this second chance we've been given."

She could feel her family practice falling to the side. Maybe not for years, but it would eventually. This was bigger, and no one else could do what she could do. No one else could give the Hellraised a fair shake.

And family practice lawyers were everywhere.

Expediency, she thought.

This is like dealing with Kyle Haversham in the restaurant. You keep the end result in mind. You remember whom you're trying to help. You never lose sight of your idealism. Then you do what you have to do to get the results you need.

She shook Puck's hand. "I'm your lawyer, Puck."

Chapter 41

Dan was still looking over the unsigned contract when Puck got home.

"I can't sign this, Puck," he said. "I can't accept money to say that I think what you're doing for the state is good. I can't become a paid spokesman for anything—that goes against what I believe in. No one can own me, or else what I say on the radio will be compromised. And what I had to say about Devil's Point would be compromised, too. If you paid me to say I thought it was a good thing, that would negate any value in what I said."

Puck dropped onto the couch and leaned back. "Long day," he said.

"I know. But don't change the subject on me."

"I'm not. It's just been a long day. Kind of hard on me." He sighed. "You're right about the contract. I'm sorry I even suggested it to Meg." He leaned forward and rested his elbows on his thighs. "You have to realize that I've spent longer than you can imagine as part of a corporate culture. The first rule of any corporation is 'Get it in writing.' The second is, 'If you aren't paying them, they don't work for you.' " He smiled wryly. "Hell doesn't exactly get a lot of free testimonials."

"Then you aren't upset?"

"Of course not. You pointed out something that would

have compromised what we're trying to do. Your point was valid, and well thought-out, and because I'm going to listen to you and take your advice, it will save us from real image problems in the near future." He chuckled. "We already have enough image problems for anyone."

Chapter 42

WEDNESDAY, JUNE 15TH

Janna got her script. She was to play an archeologist—tough, intelligent, beautiful—who, on a dig with an ex-fiancé, uncovered proof that at least one form of dinosaur lived during the time of the Minoan civilization, which was the precursor civilization to classical Greece. And she and her ex-fiancé would discover a sacred box, and unlock it, and in it find three perfectly preserved eggs. When the eggs hatched into a previously unknown form of pterodactyl, she and the ex-fiancé would be headed toward fame and fortune . . . until something went wrong.

It was a great script. The dialogue had been written by someone who'd actually heard the English language spoken, and who had a sense of humor besides. The characters were surprisingly well developed within the hundred-plus pages. The premise was a little goofy, but the writer had gone to a lot of trouble to make it logically consistent within the framework of the story. The story was good. Really good. ILM was already set up to do the special effects, which meant the pterodactyls would *live*.

It was the project she'd worked her whole life for, and she was going to star in it, and she'd just heard that Brad Pitt had tentatively agreed to play her ex-fiancé, barring scheduling conflicts. And Harrison Ford was a possible as the brilliant scientist whose work brought the pterodactyls to life.

She should have been walking on air.

Instead, she felt only a sick, tight knot in her gut. This wasn't any fun. This wasn't the way she'd wanted to do it at all. She discovered, too late, that she wouldn't be satisfied with enormous success unless she earned it—and now, with success guaranteed her, with the rest of her life mapped out and looking like the star-studded path of a goddess, with everything she wanted in the palm of her hand, she didn't see any way that she could go back to the place where she'd been before—to being the woman who was willing to work her ass off to get what she wanted if only she could know when she got to the top that she'd done it herself.

I want to know that Anton Leighton-White liked me, she thought. I want to know that I was really the actress he wanted. And I won't ever know that.

Everything I do from here on out is poisoned.

What do I do?

Chapter 43

Dan stared out his apartment window at the advancing clouds. The county had a severe weather watch until midnight—looked like they were going to get their weather. A thunderstorm would be perfect for his mood, too.

Work had sucked. He'd done riffs on Raleigh politicians, on Washington idiocy, on the local fight over banning *Huckleberry Finn* in the classroom. He wanted to talk about something different, something that wasn't devils and Hell, and every call-in he got turned him back to the Great Devil Makeover.

The press conference had sucked. Meg had stood in front of a press corps as big and interested as any that had ever showed up for a presidential State of the Union address, and had introduced the Devil's Point project, done a brief spiel about how it was going to revitalize the North Carolina economy, and launched from there into a prepared address about the ACLU antidiscrimination suit, the sufferings of the Hellraised in North Carolina, and finally into a big push for equal rights for the Hellraised.

At no time did Meg say anything about second chances, about a push toward redemption. She seemed to have forgotten that the idea had been to remake Hell's damned, because now she was agitating to get them accepted into society as they were.

Dan kept waiting for his chance to speak, for his opportunity to say that he *didn't* support equal rights for the Hellspawn, but while Meg pointed him out and people cheered, he never got a chance at the microphone.

And when the press conference was over, she'd given him a hard look and said, "I heard you decided not to join us after all. It figures that when you have a real chance to make a difference, you'd back out. A man who would string along two women wouldn't have the courage of his convictions, would he?"

He'd tried to explain, but she walked away.

He reached Janna on the phone. She told him that she'd gotten the part she'd always wanted, and that she didn't see where the two of them had a future. She would be traveling around the world. She would be famous. She wouldn't have time for a DJ boyfriend who kept worse hours than she did.

She said she wished him luck.

She sounded like she'd been crying.

Now he was alone. The storm marched up from the southwest, from the Gulf of Mexico, and he wanted to stand in it. He wanted to let it pound him flat.

He'd lost both Meg and Janna. Both of them. He'd lost them because he wouldn't let go of Francie. And maybe he wouldn't have had a real future with either of them, but he would never know that. Maybe one of the two of them had been the right woman for him. If he'd given either of them a real chance, maybe he would have found he'd been able to resurrect the part of himself that had died with his wife.

Fetch trotted into the room, and came over to stand by Dan's leg. Dan reached down and rubbed behind the imp's ears. "I brought another candy bar for you," he said. "I stuck it in the fridge because it started to melt in the car."

The imp stood looking up at him.

"You can go get it. It's on the top shelf."

The imp didn't move. It cocked its head to one side and made a curious little interrogative noise.

"What?"

The imp rested its hand on Dan's leg and suddenly he realized it was trying to let him know it was . . . concerned? About him?

The imp cared about him? At some point in its human life, it had committed a damnable offense, and it hadn't yet repented that. It was evil—by nature or by choice, and probably by both. He'd done nothing to try to give it a second chance—hadn't given it clothes or tried to find it a job or even paid it special attention. The occasional candy bar, a pat on the head, a scratch behind the ears—nothing worth mentioning.

But he could see the concern in its eyes.

"Janna and Meg both dumped me," he said. "I'm a little down."

That little interrogative squeak again.

"I'm understating. I'm a lot down. I'm discovering that I cared about both of them, and I'm discovering it too late."

It patted his leg. An attempt at comfort, and he found himself moved that it tried.

He heard a step on the stairs outside the apartment, and Fetch shot away to its corner, and rolled up into a ball there. An instant later, Puck came through the door.

"Big day," the devil said. "I think the press conference went well. Your presence made a real difference for us, Dan. Thank you for coming."

Dan shrugged.

"Really. I'm tremendously grateful. I think that having

a man of your moral fiber associated with Devil's Point will clear our obstacles faster than a flame thrower at a weenie roast."

Dan said nothing.

"That was supposed to be a joke."

"Oh. It was funny."

"I'm trying to tell you how much your presence on the platform with us today meant to me."

Dan said, "Don't worry about it." He turned back to the window and stared out at the black clouds that moved toward him. Flashes of lightning illuminated the underside of the cloud bank at irregular intervals, and the distant rumble of thunder followed after, slowly.

"You're angry."

"I'm . . . unhappy."

"Why?"

Dan looked over at the devil. He didn't seem much like a devil anymore. He'd become almost a friend. Perhaps he could become a friend—and right at that moment, Dan thought he needed a friend more than anything.

He said, "Do you have a while?"

"My evening is free."

So Dan told him about Francie; about meeting her and loving her and finally losing her. He talked until his voice grew hoarse and his throat grew raw, until the thunder and the lightning crashed all around them so close the apartment shook, and the rain slashed against the windows, and the wind outside screamed like a banshee and whistled through the gap between the front door and the frame.

And he talked on, about how he'd looked for her replacement in both Meg and Janna, and how he'd made a mistake in doing that. "No one could replace her," he said. "And I should have seen the two of them for who they were, and not as plugs for the huge hole in my life."

Puck sat, listening, not commenting at all until at last Dan fell silent. Then he said, "You truly loved her."

"She was the human embodiment of love. She was my whole world—when she died, I had to find other reasons just to keep breathing, because she'd been my reason for everything I did."

"You loved her . . ." The devil stared out at the black sky, and a close flash of lighting illuminated his face and for a moment made him almost handsome. Compassion showed clearly in his eyes, and a comprehension of Dan's pain.

"I, too, lost those I loved," Puck said at last. "My wife gave me three children, and not long after the youngest was born, she died. My oldest son died when he was eleven. My life after his death spiraled downward, into unending despair and grief. I did things that I now remember . . . and regret . . . and I did those bad things because God took away from me the people I loved."

Dan looked at the devil. "I understand," he said softly. "When Francie died, I blamed God for not saving her."

The devil nodded. "I did the same thing. And it didn't help me after I died to discover that he could have saved them, and that he let them die as a lesson to me."

Dan, startled, said, "God could have saved Francie? He really did let her die?"

"Of course. Surely that's more evident to you now than ever—if he can put us here, he can cure the dying of their cancers and diseases and sicknesses. But he sends the diseases—why would he choose to take them away?"

The anger that he'd felt when Francie died came back to Dan, washed over him like a tidal wave, and dragged him with it out to the sea of rage where he'd spent so much time just a few short years ago.

"I did realize that. I realized it when God turned all of you loose here—that miracles weren't impossible after all."

"I saved you, Dan. God could have saved her. Miracles happen."

Dan nodded. Anger swelled in his throat, a hard hot knot that made swallowing difficult and speaking impossible.

The devil said, "You didn't make a mistake in not loving Meg or Janna. They weren't right for you. Both of them had plans of their own, lives completely apart from yours. Both of them have proven that they can get by just as well without you as they can with you. And, quite frankly, neither of them love *you*. If they did, they would still be a part of your life."

Dan locked his hands together so tightly they hurt. The muscles in his arms and shoulders went tight. He'd felt this all along, but hearing someone else say it made it more real.

"No," Puck continued, "you had the one woman in all the world who was right for you. Your other half. Your true love. And God took her away from you because he felt you needed to experience that pain and loss in order to—how did God phrase that when he tried me?—ah, yes, 'in order to permit your soul to grow stronger and purer.' I lost a wife and son when a couple of college courses in philosophy could have had the same effect."

Dan stared at him, angry and miserable and lost.

The devil said softly, "God banished his wife when he grew jealous of her worshipers—there is no Goddess in Heaven now. He ordered his son killed so that he could experience the pain of loss. He's never been human, Dan. He doesn't know what it means to grieve, to be helpless, to yearn for something that no one can give you, to be willing to offer everything you have for just . . . one . . . miracle." The devil shook his head slowly. "God doesn't know. But I do. I was there. I stood in your shoes. I remember now. And I remember why I didn't repent when I had the chance. God took my family on purpose, just as he took yours."

All the old bitterness, the fury, the hatred of God and his own life, the envy of those who still had their loves, the desire for revenge in any way he could get it, flooded Dan again, as fresh and sharp and strong as those feelings had been the moment Francie breathed out and didn't breathe in again.

The tears streamed down his cheeks and he whispered, "Why couldn't he have taken me?"

"He could have, but he decided you needed to suffer more than Francie. He decided you weren't a good enough person."

"I would have given anything I had to save her. Anything."

And the devil said, "I know, Dan. I know. But would you give anything to have her back?"

Chapter 44

Honorial crouched next to the monitor that showed the devil and Dan Cooley in Dan's living room, so angry he almost couldn't form words. "He's *lying*!"

God glanced over at him. "Of course he's lying. Did you expect him to tell the truth?"

"But he's *lying* about you. He killed his own wife and child—he did terrible things to the other two. And he's blaming you for all of that. You don't give humans diseases. You don't take lovers away from each other. You gave them each other so that they wouldn't be alone always, so that their lives wouldn't be so hard. Diseases and pain and death are all a part of life—they have nothing to do with you." Honorial sputtered to a stop when he saw the strange look God was giving him.

"Honorial, do you need a vacation?"

The Data Processing angel flushed and turned away from his Creator. "Your Glorious All-Seeing All-Knowing Awesomeness, please don't mock me."

"I'm not mocking you, honest to me." God vaulted onto the half-wall that ran around part of Honorial's workspace and sat there swinging his legs and absently braiding and unbraiding a section of his beard. "I'm wondering if I've been working you too hard since I instituted Operation Tarheel. How can you possibly be surprised that he's lying to Dan? He's lied about everything from the moment the two of them met—and he arranged their meeting."

"But he was doing better! He tried to save your daughter Maralee's life in the parking lot when the bomb killed her."

"No, he didn't. He put on a good show, but had he wanted to save her, she'd still be alive."

Honorial said, "But he saved Dan's life."

"Which only proves my point about Maralee. He led both Janna and Meg into damnation—Janna through greed and laziness, Meg through idealism."

"But saving Dan's life was a good thing."

"Was it? Maybe. Maybe not. It all depends on why the devil did it. Even good things can be done for evil reasons. See how things turn out with Dan before you say that with such assurance."

Honorial frowned. "I began to hope that devil would repent. He seemed so different. He seemed so caring."

"He spent his life seeming to be something that he wasn't. I didn't expect him to change so quickly or so easily."

Chapter 45

Janna stood on the balcony of her apartment, staring down at the patio far below. In the daylight, the bed of concrete and stone was far too beautiful to do what she planned to do—with its surrounding borders of hostas and river birches and with the little black fountain in the very center, it looked like a little Garden of Eden. Had she decided to jump in daylight, she would have left a dreadful mess.

But in the blackness of the storm, the concrete was a pale flatness, amoeba-shaped, almost indistinguishable from the surrounding beds of plantings. She wouldn't have to think about her blood on the aggregate, because the pounding rain would wash away the blood. Wash away her mistakes. Wash away the future that she'd sold out from under herself. She'd take the quick road to Hell, and skip a lifetime of looking like a great success and feeling like a bitter failure.

She held the contract in her left hand, crumpled. When someone found her body, he'd find the contract with it, and people would know why she'd done what she'd done. She wasn't worried that the contract would be destroyed by the weather. The rain left Hell's paper untouched. It didn't get soggy or sodden, the letters didn't run, the corners didn't curl. That didn't surprise her. She figured if she had thrown it into a fire, it probably wouldn't have burned either.

Pity the makers of envelopes couldn't get the formula, she thought. The post office had creamed enough of her mail that she figured nothing but Hell-proof paper would get through unscathed.

Similar environments. Similar bureaucracies.

She climbed onto the white cast-iron lawn chair she kept on her balcony and stared down into the darkness. She only stood a couple feet higher than she had before, but suddenly she felt dizzy. That would pass.

She smiled a hopeless smile. So would everything else.

The wind gusted past her, buffeting her. She eyed the poured-concrete railing and swallowed. The top of the railing was about six inches wide, and the whole thing was sturdy. Still, she hesitated. The wind would make standing on that railing precarious—and she intended to jump, but she did not wish to fall. She wanted some control over the last moments of her life.

She braced both hands on the railing at the corner and scooted one leg up onto it. Then the other. The rain soaked through her clothes, stuck her hair to her face, stung her skin like a shower of BBs. It blew first left, then right, then left again as the wind shifted its patterns around the apartment building and found different routes through the complex. Lightning illuminated her target, then left her in darkness blacker than before, with afterimages of the ground below her etched in blue, white and black on her eyes.

When she could see again, she tightened her grip on the contract that stole from her everything she'd worked for, and slowly began to stand.

Chapter 46

Meg looked out into the darkness. The incubus Larial, whom she'd first met in her law office just the day before, stood beside her, one strong hand resting on the small of her back.

"The storm is magnificent," he whispered into her hair, "full of rage and power and hunger. But you would shame the storm, and make it as weak and mewling as a kitten, if you released your passion. Ah, Megan. Let me pleasure you. Let me give you all the magic in my body."

Meg felt the thunder as much as she heard it; felt the rumble in her belly, in her breasts, in the tingling of her skin. She said, "I'm your lawyer. I represent you."

"You are doing so much that is good for my kind, beautiful Meg. You'll give so much of your time and your effort to our lives. And what will you get in return? Only money? Money is cold, and it won't kiss you awake in the morning. It won't fill you, or tease you, or lick you, or bring you to ecstasy. It won't make you scream with pleasure . . . like I will."

"It won't damn me to Hell, either," she said.

"I won't damn you to Hell, Meg. Perhaps you can teach me to love. Perhaps we can find love for each other in our searches for pleasure. In Hell there is no place for love—did you know that? You didn't, did you? I can see it in your eyes."

"That's ridiculous," Meg said. "You're saying that the only people in Hell are those who don't love anyone."

"Or anything. If you truly love your work, or your hobbies, or even your pets, you can't go to Hell. Love will save you. You could save me, Meg. You know about love. You know what it is. Teach me."

Meg felt the incubus's hands cupping her breasts, sliding down her belly, undoing the clasp and zipper of her skirt. His movements were so familiar; she closed her eyes and she could imagine the hands belonged to Dan.

And anger tightened her muscles, and rage soured her stomach.

Dan, you bastard. You embarrassed me in front of my clients. In front of my uncle. You had the balls to call my house and try to enlist him in helping you make up to me. You were sleeping with some other woman while you were dating me, and even if we never said we were exclusive, I wasn't seeing anyone else.

The hands kept slipping . . . sliding . . . caressing.

"You know about love," he said in Dan's voice. "He showed you what love was."

Love, she thought. I know about love, all right. He showed me what love wasn't. And you're just like him, aren't you? You want to use me, too.

Well, it isn't going to work this time.

She turned, both angry and aroused, and ripped Larial's zipper down, and yanked his pants down around his knees. She wanted to hurt, to embarrass, to shame Dan—but Dan wasn't with her, and Larial was.

She tripped him backwards, and when he collapsed to the floor, slapped him once across the face. That was for Dan.

I can't love you, you bastard. You're just like Dan.

But I can use you.

Chapter 47

Puck held out a hand, and Dan saw a light begin to shimmer in the darkness of his living room. It formed into a rounded cylinder about five and a half feet tall, and the cylinder began to shape itself into the form of a woman. High, tight breasts, long legs, narrow waist, flowing hair the color of dark honey. Huge sad hazel eyes, narrow nose, full lips.

And the smile that he could never forget. The smile that said "I love you, and I will love you forever."

"Francie," he whispered.

She held out her arms to him and his heart felt like it would break.

"I can give her to you," Puck said.

The voice was outside of Dan's head, but inside of it too. *I can give her back to you.*

Would you give anything to have her back?

Would you give anything?

Anything?

And he thought, She's right there. Not solid yet, but she's Francie. My Francie.

And Puck is my friend. He saved my life. He cares about me.

I would give anything to have her back.

Would you?

Of course. I love her.

How much do you love her? Would you give me your soul?

That was the question, of course. He knew it was the question Puck would ask, though he didn't know how he knew. Puck had redeemed himself. Puck had saved Dan's life. He had escaped Hell, regained his memories of his past, repented . . .

But he hadn't repented. He was still angry with God for taking away his wife and his son. He still hated God for sentencing him to Hell.

And Dan had said he understood. But did he?

He'd been dead. He'd been above his body, away from the world, and he knew without a doubt that Francie would be waiting for him. He *knew* that he would find her there. Where? Certainly not in Hell. Francie had loved the whole world and everyone in it. Wherever Francie was—and Dan wasn't certain that she was in a literal Heaven with angels and harps and God with a long white beard—she was someplace good.

He'd been on his way to her.

And Puck had pulled him back.

And Puck was offering him a physical reincarnation of Francie for the few years the two of them would live. In exchange, he would give up an eternity with Francie in that wonderful place she'd discovered beyond.

Dan stared at Puck.

"You can't really give her back to me. You can only take me away from her. Can't you?"

He caught movement behind Puck. The imp, Fetch, shaking his head vehemently back and forth. No, no, no. But doing it out of Puck's line of vision.

"Don't be silly," Puck said. "She's right here. I'll have to have your signature on a few documents before I can completely materialize her—you wouldn't believe the number of Hellawatts it takes to bring someone back."

"You're right," Dan said quietly. "I wouldn't."

Puck stopped smiling. "Dan," he said, "what's gotten into you? I'm offering to give you Francie again. I can't tell you what I would have done if I'd had an offer like this. Here she is . . . the woman you love . . . and look at her, Dan. She wants you. She's waiting for you to bring her back into your arms. You think she hasn't missed you as much as you've missed her?"

Francie held out her hands to him. Pleading. Her eyes were so sad and full of longing, her tremulous smile so full of hope. His heart nearly stopped from the pain of turning away from her.

He reminded himself of the succubus he'd met, the one who'd offered to be Francie for him. He looked again to this ghostly Francie, and he wondered how much of her, if any of her, had ever been the woman he'd loved whole-heartedly. Probably none of her. Francie's soul was surely beyond the devil's reach. He couldn't haul her out of the afterlife and stuff her into a body—so this woman who looked just like Francie, and who might even act just like Francie, couldn't possibly be Francie. If she wasn't another succubus, she was something Puck had created from Dan's dreams and wishes and memories.

These Hellraised monsters were going to bring back the dodos and the dinosaurs and the woolly mammoths; they were going to have Wyatt Earp and John Lennon and Marie Antoinette walking around in their park shaking hands with the paying customers. Why in God's name would he think Puck couldn't create a convincing replica of Francie?

That's when it all became clear.

Resolutely he turned back to Puck and said, "Now I know why you saved my life."

Puck's eyebrows rose. "You do? Well, I'm glad to

hear that. I saved your life because I'm your friend."

"No," Dan said. "You saved my life because if I'd died then, I would have gone to be with Francie, and I would have been beyond your reach. You saved my life because I wasn't damned yet."

Puck laughed.

"You've been working on me all along, haven't you? You're no closer to redemption now than you were when I met you."

Puck continued laughing, and he began to change. He grew taller, broader, uglier. His skin sprouted scales and his forehead and shoulders sprouted horns and his fingers changed to razor-tipped claws. Hellish fangs slid out of increasingly heavy jaws. His clothes vanished, and two black leathery wings unfurled from his back. His laughter got deeper and uglier.

"Why would I want to repent?" he asked. "Why would any of the Hellraised want to repent? We have power. We have wealth. We have unimaginable knowledge. We can do things you can't even begin to understand."

"Get out, Puck," Dan said.

"And leave you without your darling Francie? You're damned anyway now, Dan. Damned and doubly damned. Because of how you treated her, Meg is at this very moment fornicating with an incubus, knowing full well what it is, and not caring. She's hating you and cursing you for your infidelity, and swearing that she'll never forgive you. That sort of hatred would be enough to damn her, and would be almost enough to take you down with her; those who cause the damnation of others are themselves damned. But that's not all."

Dan closed his eyes. He could almost sense what the devil was about to say.

"Right now Janna is standing on her balcony railing, getting ready to take the big plunge, if you know what

I mean. She's realized that you don't really love her, Danny boy, and she thinks it's the only way out."

"You're lying," Dan said between clenched teeth. "You're full of shit!"

Puck shrugged, and described a circle in the air with one claw. The inside of the circle turned white, and then Dan saw Janna, just as Puck said, standing on the balcony railing, her hair whipping violently in the wind.

Is it a trick? he thought. Could he show me this if it weren't really happening?

"There's something else," Puck said. He waved his hand and the image of Janna disappeared. "She's carrying your child, Dan. She's carrying your child and soon the two of them will be nothing more than a wet spot on the pavement. And it will be your fault."

The devil laughed.

"And tomorrow my people are going to make sure that the Great Devil Makeover is proven to be a fraud. I'm going to go out and show them how I really am. And *who* I really am. My name is Scumslag, and I'm in charge of Satco. I'm going to lay out all the contracts I've signed with your radio station clients—you think they wanted to talk to me because I knew where their relatives were? They wanted deals—wealth, power, success, a longer life. All of them signed my contracts. And you were with me, so how is anyone ever going to believe that you weren't in on it—on this attempt to defraud and deceive an entire nation?"

"No," Dan said. "They wanted reassurance."

"They wanted what only I could give them. Guaranteed success. You know what else? Because of you, we got the land we wanted to build Devil's Point. All because of you. We figure we can get more souls out of Devil's Point in a month than we got in ten years by regular methods. And the other devils who've been taken in and cared for by all you suckers are going to come out and let everyone see the souls they've collected. Because of you, Dan. Because of you, and the good thing you did, helping a poor unfortunate devil find his way back to Heaven."

The devil tapped on the table with one claw. "Every soul that's damned because you helped us will count against you in the Old Communist's record books. Millions of souls."

The devil smiled an evil smile. "Pretty good thing you did there, wasn't it? You fooled a nation and damned some of the better people in the state, and come tomorrow you aren't going to be able to lift your head. They'll be hunting for it from here to Alaska. So take Francie now. Sign my contract and take her, because you'll never see her again after you die. Your soul already belongs to us. All my contract will do now is dictate the terms of your service to Hell. And maybe let you live a little longer when they come hunting for you—after all, we take care of our own."

Lightning turned the room white. Thunder shook the walls and the floor and rattled the dishes.

It could all be true, Dan thought. Perhaps none of the Hellraised had escaped the clutches of Hell; maybe, as Puck—rather, Scumslag—said, they didn't want to.

Maybe every good thing I intended to do has done evil instead.

The road to Hell is paved with good intentions.

And maybe it was all just a lie to get Dan to sign the contract. The imp still stood back there in the corner, shaking his head. No. No. No.

Dan looked up to the place where he always figured Heaven would be, and he said, "God, if I've screwed this up, I'm sorry. I mean really, really sorry. I only wanted to help the Hellraised take advantage of the second chance you gave them. Please don't let anything bad happen to Janna, or to Meg. Please."

He meant it with everything in him.

He didn't expect what happened next. Scumslag screamed and vanished. "Francie" howled, metamorphosed into a hideous long-fanged gray-scaled monster out of a nightmare, and shimmered into darkness.

Several sheets of paper fell to the floor, where they exploded on contact, burned brightly for just an instant without catching anything else on fire, and left the room in darkness.

He stood shaking. "I have to call Meg," he said. "And Janna—Christ, I have to save Janna. I have to let them know."

He heard the scuffling of tiny feet, and felt a tug at his pants leg. In a raspy, barely audible voice Fetch said, "Come too?"

Chapter 48

Janna stood on the railing, her arms outstretched, the contract in her hand.

She squinted into the rain that slashed across her face, feeling herself swaying with the wind.

I blew it, God, she thought. *I was a jerk and a creep; I used people; I was probably at least halfway to Hell before I signed the contract, and I'm sorry I did it. I'm sorry. If I had it to do over, I'd do it differently, but it's too late for me now.*

She took a deep breath.

Too late for me.

The contract in her hand burst into flames.

Startled, shocked, she flung it away from her, lost her balance, and fell. Backward. Over the chair. Onto her balcony, where she lay on the concrete with her head ringing and aching and her ribs on fire from the place where they'd hit the chair on the way down. She watched the contract burn.

The rain stopped.

She looked up at the black sky, and a flash of lighting illuminated the clouds. She almost expected to see God looking down at her, but she saw only the rounded underbellies of the cumulonimbus clouds that scudded by, racing toward the sea.

The thunder rumbled.

Shaking, hurting, she sat up. Her contract with Hell had burst into flames when she'd said she was sorry. She was free. Her entire life lay before her, and if she didn't have guaranteed success in it, she had an endless stream of opportunities. She would make of them what she could.

She drew herself to her feet, and realized something was thudding against her front door. She wobbled a little as she hurried to answer it.

It burst open before she got there, and Dan charged in, shouted, "Christ, you're alive," and threw his arms around her.

She stood there like an idiot, with tears running down her cheeks. She wrapped her wet arms around him and sobbed. "I'm alive," she said. "I'm alive."

They held each other for the longest time, and when they pulled apart, she could see that he'd been crying as hard as she had.

"I haven't been completely honest with you," he said, stroking her hair. "There are some things in my past I need to tell you about. I was married once. My wife died of cancer. I promised myself when she died that I'd never fall in love again—that it hurt too much. But that's no way to live. It's like dying with her. And I'm not ready to die."

"Me either." She nodded. "I've kept my own secrets, too, Dan. I've used people, I've lied, I've done things to hurt people who never did anything to me. I may not be perfect in the future, but I'll be better. I've seen the other side."

"Do we have a chance together?" he asked her.

She looked at his face, imagining the two of them growing old together. Not a very Hollywood image—but she could see it. More importantly, she could believe it. "We have a chance. Not a guarantee, you know—"

He smiled. "A guarantee would be too easy."

She took his hands in hers, and nodded. She deserved better than guarantees.

He asked her, "Are you pregnant?"

Her eyes went wide. "Of course not. Why would you think that?"

"Something Puck said—that you were killing yourself and our baby because of me."

"No. Because of my own stupidity. Because I signed a deal with the devil, and thought that meant I couldn't repent. But it's never too late to repent."

"Not ever."

Something brushed against her leg. Something small, and furry. She looked down expecting to see the kitten—and indeed the little monster still had its kitten body—but its head had transformed into something hideous. Green, toothy, with glowing red eyes and mucus dripping from the cavernous nostrils, it grinned at her, then hissed.

She yelped, and Dan saw the little monster, and grabbed it, and chucked it off the balcony in one quick toss.

She shuddered, perhaps from standing in the air conditioning wearing soaking wet clothes, or perhaps from that last reminder of where she had been, and what had nearly become of her. She whispered, "A gift from Puck."

"I almost ended up with one of those myself," Dan said, and hugged her closer.

Chapter 49

Lucifer tightened the rack another notch. Scumslag, long past coherent reply, gave another inarticulate scream as parts of his body crunched and ripped.

"Do you have any idea how many of my people your little experiment cost me?" Lucifer asked. "Eighty-three percent of your hand-picked volunteers turned." Lucifer gave the crank another turn. "Eighty-three percent. In exchange for over two thousand of my best Hellraised workers, do you know how many souls we got that we wouldn't have had otherwise?"

Crank.

Scream.

"One."

Crank.

Scream.

"I got Meg Lerner out of it—and maybe I'll be able to hang onto her until she dies. But she might get smart, too. It isn't like I can send someone up there to kill her off while she's still ours."

Crank.

Scream.

"This is not good, Scumslag. Not good at all. You can consider this the first notice of your demotion."

Crank.

Scream.

"You got me the ground for Devil's Point. I'll give you that. More than anything else, that's why I'm being so easy on you."

Crank.

Scream.

Crank.

Scream.

"But who am I going to find to build it? And to run it? Who could possibly be more evil than you? Where else am I going to find someone with an MBA *and* an Evilness Index of 970?"

Lucifer stared off into the gloomy reaches of Hell as he gave the crank a final turn. He thought about the future. A smile began to tug at the corners of his mouth, and he leaned in close to his former away-commander.

"I'll find someone, I suppose. I have to. I can't let our grand opportunity go to waste. After all," he said quietly. "There is so much left to do." He gently traced one talon across Scumslag's sweat-beaded forehead.

And then he began the torture.